A VERY PRIVATE WOMAN

CONNOR WHITELEY

No part of this book may be reproduced in any form or by any electronic or mechanical means. Including information storage, and retrieval systems, without written permission from the author except for the use of brief quotations in a book review.

This book is NOT legal, professional, medical, financial or any type of official advice.

Any questions about the book, rights licensing, or to contact the author, please email connorwhiteley@connorwhiteley.net

Copyright © 2023 CONNOR WHITELEY

All rights reserved.

DEDICATION

Thank you to all my readers without you I couldn't do what I love.

CHAPTER 1
1ˢᵗ April 2022
Canterbury, England

"Why don't you get a real job sis?"

Private Eye Bettie English was really starting to learn very quickly that people loved to put pregnant women down. She didn't understand why just because she was pregnant her own sister felt the need to force her (not that she would ever admit it) to give up what she loved, and was extremely good at.

As Bettie sat at her wonderfully warm wooden desk with her laptop open and a large mug of water (that she was pretending was amazingly strong coffee), all she could do was just sit there and nod along to whatever her sister Phryne was saying.

To completely stop her sister from accusing Bettie of not paying attention, Bettie stared into her little green eyes, and Bettie had to admit that Phryne didn't look her best today.

Normally she wore the so-called latest fashion

trends. Including a rather amazing range of haircuts, skirts and even new types of jeans over the decades. But today she looked completely different.

Bettie had no idea how to describe it, but when she told her boyfriend about it all later. She would probably go with calling it "the common street people look". Not that Bettie actually looked much better in her oversized black t-shirt, jeans and trainers.

She was pregnant after all. She was focusing on giving birth to a kid, not her fashion choices.

But as the sound of the students on the high street below, the singing of birds and her sister's talking all grew louder and louder. Bettie was definitely going to ask her boyfriend to give her a foot massage later.

Probably to his utter horror, but he loved her, and she him.

As much as Bettie loved her sister (that was twenty years older than her) and all the so-called wisdom of her upbringing, raising her own children. Bettie just didn't want to put up with all the nonsense about how she had to stay at home for the next five years to make sure the kid got a good upbringing

Bettie just didn't want to hear it.

Her office and her Private Eye work was her amazing escape. Bettie loved helping people, solving crimes and improving lives.

Why would she give it up?

Bettie and her boyfriend Graham had already decided that neither one of them was going to leave their jobs. But they both wanted this kid to have the best childhood possible.

And Bettie was damn well going to make sure that happened.

The hints of flowers, sugar and perfume hit Bettie's senses as her sister started to wave her arms about, kicking her perfume into the air. Bettie forced herself not to gag at the strong smell. The hints didn't smell awful in the slightest, but as she had learnt a lot recently, her body was a lot more sensitive to smells than it use to be.

"So you need to give up your hobby, and get a real job. There's a new position opening up in my place," Phryne said.

Bettie forced herself not to swear. She might have loved her sister, just not enough to work with her.

"This isn't a hobby," Bettie said, "I am a Private Eye, I investigate crimes and I am licensed by the British Private Eye Federation. That wasn't easy!"

Phryne shook her head. "Seriously Sis. You have a hobby Federation. That's sad,"

Bettie's mouth just fell open. She knew there was no winning with her sister, and she really wanted her gone. She had plenty of business to take care of, including a mountain of new background checks to perform for big companies.

"You work for Knight And King, right?" Bettie asked.

"Of course," Phryne said. "I am Senior Manager

for the Law Firm after my recent change,"

"And you're getting a lot of interns, new recruits and other people at the moment. Including 631 new interns starting on the 16th May," Bettie said.

Phryne's eyes widened. "How did you know that? This is most unprofessional Bettie. That is strictly-"

Bettie waved her sister silent and spun her laptop around which showed that she had the contract for checking out all new recruits that the company was hiring.

"Now my darling sis," Bettie said with a smile, "My door is over there. Please close it when you go out, because I clearly have a lot to do in my little hobby,"

Phryne didn't look like she knew what to say, so Bettie just pointed to the door again. She was even tempted to show her sister how much money the company was paying her for each background check, but she wasn't that evil.

Yet.

Someone knocked on the door three times.

Bettie just looked at Phryne. "Someone for you?"

Phryne shrugged. "I thought this was another hobby person of yours,"

Bettie was so tempted to throw a pencil at her sister.

The person knocked again.

"Come in!" Bettie shouted, and felt the little guy inside her kick a little. That warmed Bettie's heart.

The massive wooden door to the office started

banging against the frame.

"What?" Phryne asked, clearly as confused as Bettie about why the person wasn't coming in.

Bettie gestured to her baby bump. "Help the person in please,"

Phryne nodded and opened the door. A second later a really tall young man walked in dressed in a black tracksuit, black trainers and some kind of gold necklace.

Just from looking at him Bettie instantly knew he wasn't looking for a private eye. Those people always looked more alert and like they know roughly what they're after.

This guy didn't look like he had a clue. Bettie would actually be surprised if he knew how to tie up his own shoe laces.

"Can I help you?" Bettie asked.

The guy slowly looked at her, and looked stunned and really confused as soon as he saw the baby bump.

"Are ya Bettie English? The Private Eye?" he said, clearly unsure of just about everything.

"I am," Bettie said.

"And I'm her sister Phryne. Do you need any legal advice?"

Bettie couldn't believe her sister was trying to get customers herself in front of her. That was outrageous.

"Na," the man said, "my boss needs you to come with me. She... They want to see you,"

Bettie subtly looked at Phryne. Thankfully her sister sat back down.

"Who's your boss?" Bettie asked.

"Not allowed to say," the man said.

"Why not?" Bettie said.

"Not allowed to say," the man said.

"Who are you?" Phryne said.

"Not allowed to say," the man said.

Normally Bettie would just turn this man away instantly, because there was something clearly weird about him. But she did want to prove to her sister how good of a private eye she was, and this weirdo might be the way to do it.

But she did need to think of the baby and Graham, Bettie was going to have to be careful.

"Sorry," Bettie said. "Unless I know your employer, I am not going,"

The man muttered something and started to pace around.

"Well," he said, "my boss said to bring you no matter what,"

Bettie carefully moved her hand under her desk to where she always kept a knife for such occasions.

"So I think it's okay for me to reveal who is," the man said.

Bettie let out a breath she didn't know she was holding.

"She is Mrs Willow Fisher," the man said.

"Wow!" Phryne shouted.

Bettie had no clue who this woman was, she was

clearly important judging by the look on her sister's face. She hadn't seen Phryne this happy since her son Sean and his boyfriend had bought her tickets to some awful concert.

Bettie was more than glad she didn't have to go.

"Who is she?" Bettie asked.

"Oh you are so… small minded," Phryne said.

Bettie had never been called that before. She was shocked.

"She's a legendary lawyer. She actually inspired me and my career change. She was an author who wrote so many self-help books,"

As much as Bettie wanted to run and hide from this problem, because in Bettie's experience, self-help people were always over-the-top, and if they write books then they probably think of themselves as god's gift to humanity.

Bettie didn't need that.

But she was a private eye first and foremost, she did this job because it was extremely fun, she loved solving mysteries and helping people.

And there was a person in need who wanted Bettie's help, and she was going to give it.

"On one condition," Bettie said. She didn't need to mention her fees yet (and her increasing them because of the strangeness of it all).

"What?" the man said.

Bettie looked at Phryne and smiled at how excited she was getting.

"My sister comes too,"

Phryne jumped up and down in happiness. Bettie just wasn't sure if she was going to regret this case.

She had a feeling she would.

CHAPTER 2
1st April 2022
Canterbury, England

There was nothing more than Detective Graham Adams hated more than dirty disgusting criminals using young women to do their dirty work for them.

After spending the night in his cold dark little car, Graham was less than impressed with these criminals. He was still freezing this morning as the cold English morning was never going to warm up until much, much later.

And he flat out hated the coldness.

As Graham looked out down the street with large houses either side of it, he was just waiting patiently (very thin patience but still) for someone to come out a little white brick house just in front of him.

Graham would have much preferred to be spending time with his beautiful, sexy girlfriend Bettie. He wanted to hug, love and kiss her last night, and hopefully talk baby stuff because it was less than six months now.

He was just as scared as her, but the amazing thing that Graham loved about Bettie was her ability to make herself look so confident. Graham was nowhere near that skillfully.

He was so nervous about the baby, making sure he was a good dad and everything else that he had been shaking awfully at home. Whenever he saw the baby bump, he got nervous about what it meant.

As much as Graham wanted to be a dad, after his bad experience as a kid, he was terrified of getting it wrong for his own child.

The cold morning air with hints of car fumes, oranges and dry pine filled the air that left the wonderful taste of orange tarts on his tongue. As the street started to flare to life and people started to move. Graham really hoped that his criminals would get moving in a moment.

The criminals were apparently your everyday drug dealers that were using the local university students to move the drugs into clubs, universities and everywhere they wanted.

Graham couldn't care less about the university students themselves. They were just young silly people, making a bad choice. It didn't make them bad people, it only meant they had made a single silly choice.

What Graham really wanted to know was who was supplying the university students, and that had led him to this little house.

The sound of cars gently driving past, and people talking and joking with each other filled the air as Graham concentrated on a large white van that was slowly moving down the street.

Graham reached over for his police radio that he always kept under his seat and he called it in.

"This is detective Adams. A white van is coming down and now stopping outside the target house,"

Graham watched the white van park perfectly and three young men dressed in black tracksuits got out.

The radio buzzed. "Detective Adams? What are you doing out? And what's this about a target house?"

Graham swore under his breath. His friends at the police station might be some of the best detectives in the country, but they were next to useless when it came to paperwork.

Graham had specifically filed everything needed to get support (and most importantly get paid) for this overnight stakeout, but oh no, they clearly had never filed it. Or even notified the police radio people.

The three young men started to unload large cardboard boxes out of the white van.

Graham picked up the radio. "This is Detective Adams. I need backup and a crime scene unit at my location now,"

"Reason?" someone on the radio asked.

"I'm about to perform a drug bust under probable cause," Graham said, putting down the radio.

"En route," the radio said, "but please Detective wait for back up to arrive. It is five minutes out,"

The young men placed the boxes outside the little house and went back into their van.

"We don't have five minutes,"

Graham got out of the car and quickly walked down the street checking out the house numbers as he went to make sure he didn't look like a cop.

He heard the white van turn on its engine.

Graham walked over to the white van and pretended to look lost and like he was looking for a particular house. Graham turned and knocked on the white van's window.

When the young men opened their windows, Graham coughed as the extremely strong smell of weed filled the air, and Graham just gagged.

"What ya want old man?" the driver asked.

"I was wondering if you know where number 59 is?" Graham asked.

The young men frowned. "Fuck off cop,"

The men threw something at Graham.

Hitting his head.

Graham went down.

The van sped off.

Graham picked up the oddly shaped piece of rock they had thrown at him and smiled. The surface was completely smooth and he even thought he could see fingerprints.

A few seconds later the sound of sirens just made

Graham shake his head as his friends had arrived too late, and Graham knew exactly what would be in those cardboard boxes.

Plenty of weed, cocaine and heroin just like these criminals liked.

As the two police cars parked and Graham saw the crime scene techs coming down the road to process the drugs and whatever they found, Graham felt his stomach tighten into a painful knot.

With his own kid coming and after Bettie's wonderful nephew Sean being at a local university, Graham felt such a responsibility to stop these criminals. He had to stop them and stop these drugs flowing into the local area.

He had to protect the innocent people that were losing their lives every day to these criminals.

Graham just had to.

And the idea of him failing, absolutely terrified him.

CHAPTER 3
1st April 2022
Unknown Location, Somewhere Outside Canterbury, England

As soon as Bettie got out of the black jeep, she instantly wasn't impressed with wherever they had bought her and her sister too.

The sound of the gravel crunching under her feet made Bettie frown as she looked at the massive old Tudor-style house in the middle of nowhere. The white walls and massive black wooden beams that were so characteristic of this type of English house was rather nice, but it was the isolation that Bettie found so strange.

She couldn't hear a single car, lorry or even the motorway that you could always, always hear in Canterbury. Bettie had no idea where they were and considering the man who had collected them had allowed Bettie to send a single text message before taking both their phones, alarm bells were going off.

Normally Bettie drove out to a client's house herself, told a few people where she was heading and did everything a normal, sensible person did to make sure people would know where to look in case things went wrong.

Thankfully Bettie had told Graham through that single text message that she was off to see Willow Fisher with Phryne, but besides from that if things went very wrong.

She was scared about her boyfriend's ability to find and ultimately save her.

But as Bettie focused on the massive Tudor-style house in the middle of nowhere and even the "gardens" around it looking untamed, she knew she was just overreacting.

The smell of fresh air, pine and Sweet-peas were a wonderful smell to Bettie and it was like the smell provided her with the soothing and very frank contrast to the isolation, and just plain creepiness to it all.

Bettie hated places in the middle of nowhere, and now she really wasn't sure if she should have taken the case.

"Oh wow!" Phryne shouted.

Bettie watched her sister stomp around the gravel pathway and she instantly knew that she was going to be a problem. Bettie was always a Private eye that meant professionalism and business before, anything else, but she was a sister first, and an expected mother too.

Bettie wasn't sure if things went wrong, if she would be able to save everyone. She wanted to. She really, really wanted to. But she had her doubts.

The sound of wood creeping made Bettie focus on the large highly-decorated front door as it opened and out came a small elderly man wearing a tight black suit, white gloves and black shoes.

He had to be the butler.

Bettie instantly knew that all her fears were true. This Willow Fisher was clearly one of those rich, rich self-help authors who prided themselves on being the centre of attention, perfect flawless personality and just a massive pain the arse.

But Bettie had to be professional.

The Butler completely dismissed Phryne as she tried to introduce herself and Bettie stood up straight as the man smiled at her.

"Miss English. It is a pleasure, an absolute pleasure," he said.

"Thank you for the rather… strange invitation," Bettie said with a smile.

"I can only offer my apologies my dear. Mistress Fisher is a… character. May I take your luggage?"

Bettie and Phryne just looked at each other. She had no idea they needed to bring luggage.

The man in the black tracksuit got out of the car at last.

"Na these two birds don't need luggage. I didn't tell them that bit," he said.

"Mr Harman," the butler said, "please use formal

language in front of guests, the Mistress and most importantly me,"

"Yes Sir," Mr Harman said.

Bettie focused on Mr Harman, there was something about how he said Sir. She couldn't be sure, but Bettie could have sworn he served in the military at some point.

That little fact didn't help calm her down in the slightest. In her experience, wealthy people never just had former military people in their employment for the fun of it, there was normally a much more annoying reason.

"Excuse me," Bettie said, "can you please tell me why we are here?"

The Butler smiled. "Miss English, I am afraid I do not know myself. I was told to welcome you. Mr Harman was told to collect you. The housekeeper Mrs Lewis was told to feed you,"

Bettie slowly nodded. There had to be a reason.

"But Miss English, Mistress Fisher had not told us why you are here. That is for a very simple reason,"

Bettie nodded harder.

"It is because Mistress Fisher is a very private woman,"

Bettie smiled. She had dealt with very private people before, and they were actually a lot of fun to watch. Because they were so strange, eccentric and just weird.

Bettie was excited about seeing this Willow

Fisher. It was probably going to be very eye-opening for Phryne, who was now quietly talking on the phone.

As much as Bettie wanted to snatch that phone away from Phryne, she didn't. She had a feeling she would know who was on the phone very soon, before it was taken away from them.

"And why can't we have our phones?" Bettie asked.

"Due to Miss English, Mistress Fisher is a very private woman, and each of you are allowed to perform one phone call or electronic communication before we take them,"

"We will get them back though, right?" Bettie asked.

She had just renewed her phone contract for the next two years without insurance. She wasn't going to have some idiot take her phone and lose it.

"Of course Miss English. The moment you are done. You get your phone back," the Butler said.

"Thank you," Bettie said.

"Brilliant!" Phryne shouted as she handed her phone to Mr Harman.

Then Bettie really wished she hadn't bought her sister, as Phryne elegantly walked over to the Butler, took his hand and kissed it.

"Mr Butler," Phryne said.

Bettie rolled her eyes. That really wasn't his name, but she did have to find out.

"My name is Phryne and I am a Senior manager

at a local law firm, and I have just had approval from the Board of Directors to make your Mistress a very exclusive offer,"

Wow!

Bettie seriously couldn't believe her sister was trying to use her case or her so-called hobby to further herself. She always thought sisters were meant to be there for each other and support one another.

That was apparently the last thing Phryne wanted to do.

"Thank you Miss Phryne. I will deliver your message to the Mistress in time. Yet I am afraid right now, your sister is far more important,"

Bettie could only smile at that.

Phryne tapped the Butler on the shoulder. "But I am from a real law firm. We handle some of the UK's largest legal cases and we are world famous. What could my sister possibly offer you that I cannot?"

The Butler smiled at Bettie, and Bettie was rather glad he was on her side.

"Your sister is famous in the Private Eye world. I first heard of her last night in a trip to Scotland. Those Private eyes were enjoying your sister's success, it is a shame her own family do not,"

Then Bettie simply followed the Butler into the house with Mr Harman and Phryne close behind her.

But Bettie would always remember the iconic look of shock, horror and rage in her sister's face as she learnt that Bettie was a lot more famous than her.

And Bettie loved that!

CHAPTER 4
1ˢᵗ April 2022
Canterbury, England

Graham stood in a long dark blue corridor outside two large silver doors as he waited for the Senior Crime Scene Tech to come out and tell him what she had found.

The immense smell of harsh cleaning chemicals that made the corridor stink of oranges, lemons and cloves left the rather interesting taste of fruit cake form on Graham's tongue. He knew that Bettie would hate it here, and he doubted her body could cope with it.

Graham was definitely going to have to make sure he wasn't smelling too much of the chemicals when he went home. The last thing he wanted was to make Bettie uncomfortable.

There was something always strange and even a little unnerving about waiting here. There were medical examiners, forensic specialists and tons of other people in all the different rooms that led off the corridor.

Graham had never really been too bothered about the few dead bodies he had worked on. He always hated those cases, and it always took him a long few days to get over them, but he just about managed.

That was probably one of the few advantages to Graham that he was sort of a Floating Officer. The head of Kent Police didn't tie him down to any one department, so Graham was allowed to float between depending on where his skills, experience and crime-solving abilities were needed.

Sadly they were needed on drug cases for now. Graham still hated the department, not because of the officers in the slightest. But because of the awful drug dealers and suppliers that were ruining so many lives.

The sound of high heels tapping on the other side of the silver doors made Graham stand up straight and a few seconds later a tall rather beautiful woman walked over in a long white lab coat and smiled at him.

Graham coughed slightly as her flowery perfume hit him. It was strong but Graham supposed it had to be to compete with the harsh cleaning chemicals.

"It's been too long Detective Adams," the woman said, "What department do they have you working in these days?"

Graham smiled at her. Senior Forensic Specialist Zoey Quill was one of the brightest minds he knew, she certainly knew the answer already.

"The drugs you're testing and the stone?" Graham asked.

Zoey nodded. "Interesting things your criminals have. I have never seen such… creative things used to cut the coke and heroin,"

"More or less deadly than the usual?" Graham asked.

"You know by now Detective, it is all as deadliest or not as the users, well, use it. But I don't recommend cutting coke with washing powder and flour,"

Graham just shook his head. He always hated these sorts of conversations because he wouldn't imagine why someone would want to breathe in some of these things.

"Traceable?" Graham asked.

Zoey shook her head. "No. Normal everyday flour, washing powder and there are no particles in the mixture that would tell me where they were made,"

Graham rolled his eyes. That would be way too easy.

"If the drugs were made in a factory, I would be able to detect rust or something. But there are no particles whatsoever here,"

Graham nodded. At least he knew for sure that the drugs wouldn't be helpful, he just hoped the fingerprints and the rock would be better.

"Fingerprints?" Graham asked.

Zoey's face lit up. "Well you normally can't get fingerprints off cardboard and the other materials you bought us. But I got us a new toy and-"

Graham gently placed his hands on Zoey's shoulders. "You know you're one of my favourites, but please get to the point,"

"Of course, Sorry,"

Graham nodded and took his hands away.

"It turns out we have five partial prints. I ran them through the system and got no matches. If you bring me a set of prints, I can match them for you. But the ball is in your court Detective,"

Graham smiled at that. He loved that the forensic people and the police were like some weird couple, one couldn't exist or do anything without the other.

"I'll whack the ball back over soon, I hope,"

Zoey nodded and she led Graham down the hallway away from the silver doors.

"The rock?" Graham asked.

"Ha," Zoey said. "That will be helpful. Again there were fingerprints. I cannot match them for anything. But the rock itself was interesting,"

Graham just rolled his eyes. He had no idea how a rock could be interesting. As far as he was concerned, rocks were just things people fell over, and in his experience, naturally made weapons to throw at officers.

"Come on Graham, they are interesting," Zoey said.

Graham shrugged and gestured her to stop as he reached the door leaving the forensic section of the building. They both stopped.

"This isn't a normal type of rock. I've emailed you the name, but this isn't granite, chalk or anything you would find in the local area. The rock's from Asia,"

Graham's eyebrows rose.

"How did an Asian rock attack me?"

"I'll even help you out a little more. The rock had a serial number on it, and you'll never guest to whom the rock belonged to,"

Graham smiled. "Where?"

"Your nephew's university. Or their Geology department to be precise,"

Graham gave her a half-smile.

"What's wrong? I thought you and Bettie liked using your nephew as a source,"

Graham opened his mouth but closed it. That was normally the case, but after last night, there wasn't too much normal about that.

Zoey looked around, made sure the coast was clear and stepped closer to Graham.

"What's wrong Graham?"

Graham shrugged. "My nephew isn't happy with me at the moment,"

"Please tell me you didn't make a homophobic joke," Zoey said.

Graham smiled as he could categorically say that didn't happen. He realised sometimes his jokes went too far about Sean before, and he really worked hard to make their relationship better.

Graham was far, far from homophobic and he couldn't care less about Sean being gay or his boyfriend. He loved them both.

"No but last night I told Bettie, Sean and her sister about a cop I worked with who searched a gay kid recently,"

Zoey covered her mouth with her hands. "I heard of this incident. Did that other cop explicitly target that kid because he looked gay and gave him a very public and humiliating drug search?"

Graham could only nod and Zoey just looked at him. She had heard the story already, Graham could have stopped it. He was technically more senior than that officer so he could have stopped it all.

But Graham didn't. He allowed that poor kid to be strip-searched in front of all his school friends and other students, people took photos and everything. And Graham just let it happen, he didn't know what he was scared of. Yet he was still scared and he didn't stop another officer from abusing his power.

Graham knew it was probably because the police would have punished him, or told him off going against the so-called Policing Family.

But Sean was furious with Graham.

And Graham couldn't blame him.

"Call him. Make things right," Zoey said.

"Thank you," Graham said as Zoey went into another room and Graham left the forensic section.

He knew he had to fix fences and prove to Sean that him and other officers didn't hate his "kind", but Graham had to solve a crime too.

He just wasn't sure which was more important.

And that pained him.

CHAPTER 5
1st April 2022

Unknown Location, Somewhere On The Outskirts of Canterbury, England

As soon as Bettie went into the Tudor-style house, she saw a rather wonderful living area with a wide range of expensive art hanging off the ancient walls, a large wooden staircase in the centre and any number of doors leading off into different parts of the house.

The entire place smelt old, musty and covered in varnish. It was almost enough to make Bettie gag but luckily she could tell just from the smell that the vanish wouldn't hurt the baby.

That was her only priority.

The Butler stopped in front of the staircase and gave Bettie and her sister an overdramatic gesture to show off the impressiveness of the house, and then Mr Harman offered to take their coats.

They weren't wearing any.

But Bettie was curious about the house. From everything Phryne had told her in the car about how amazing Willow Fisher was, Bettie would have expected more.

More colour, more smells and more self-help crap lying around the house. But there was nothing.

If Bettie had broken into the house, she would have imagined a little old lady lived here. Not some so-called self-help millionaire. There had to be something else going on, after all, in Bettie's experience people who had money always showed it off.

And Bettie had no reason to believe this Willow person would be any different.

Then the sound of monks singing echoed around the entire house, and Bettie just frowned as she noticed the speakers in the corners of the room. She expected this sort of chanting or music from monks in Buddhist temples (great people) but not in a house.

Then one of the doors opened and a large woman came her wearing a black apron and a wooden spoon that was dripping some food on the wood. She had a face like thunder, and Bettie had a feeling they were going to get shouted at for just turning up.

"These two the brats the Mistress wanted?" the woman half-asked, half-shouted.

"Mrs Lewis, this is Bettie English and her Sister Phryne,"

Phryne was about to walk forward and do

something silly, but Bettie held out her arm and stopped her dead.

Bettie watched as Mrs Lewis huffed and muttered and puffed before she left through the doorway. But not before the delicious smells of bacon, roast hog and other amazing meats filled the air.

Bettie leant on her sister as she gagged and coughed. Ever since falling pregnant Bettie couldn't stand the smell or sight of meat or anything from an animal, so she already knew this was going to be a difficult case.

Phryne rubbed her back gently.

"Is everything okay Miss English?"

"Yes, thank you. It's just the baby," Bettie said.

"Mr Jones!" a woman shouted from upstairs.

The butler smiled and gave Bettie and Phryne a little bow.

"Please excuse me ladies. Please wait here and I'll collect you in a moment,"

Bettie nodded and frowned as she watched him elegantly walk up the stairs. There was something off about all of this, she wasn't some weak-willed person to be ordered about. She wanted to be here for a reason.

And she felt like she was about to get it.

Yet what was bothering Bettie was how everything seemed perfect for such a place. There wasn't a depressed mood, broken windows or anything that would suggest to Bettie that a crime had been committed.

Bettie wouldn't be surprised if this self-help person just made it all up.

"Isn't this amazing!" Phryne shouted.

"Considering is just my hobby apparently. This is a rather normal day," Bettie said.

"I am sorry about that,"

"No you aren't," Bettie said.

"True. But your hobby does have some cool advantages,"

Bettie just wanted to kick her sister out, but she knew if anything went wrong then Phryne was her only hope. No matter had much that option terrified her.

"This is Miss English, Mistress," Mr Jones said.

Bettie looked up and smiled as she saw Mr Jones and a woman come down the stairs.

Bettie wasn't sure what to make of the new woman. She was clearly the one in charge with her smooth face, grey hair and expensive dress, but there was such an aura of despair around her.

Normally Bettie never believed in such things, but it was like with each step the woman took, the sadder the room got.

The woman stopped on the final step so she was taller than Bettie and she smiled.

"Miss English, it is a pleasure to meet you. I am-"

"Oh my god!" Phryne shouted. "You're Willow Fisher!"

Bettie just covered her face in her hands. This

wasn't going to go down well.

"Miss English!" Willow shouted. "I requested you to come. Not some... some woman!"

Bettie nodded. "Mistress Fisher, this is my sister Phryne. She's... a big fan,"

"Seriously? Miss English this is an important matter. I do not need such distractions. I am a very private woman after all. I trust your discretion. I do not others,"

Bettie was rather liking this case so far. It seemed like everyone loved her, and hated her sister. She could get use to that.

"My apologies Mistress," Bettie said. "What is this all about?"

Willow frowned at Phryne and gestured Bettie to come close. Bettie did and she saw Mr Harman stop Phryne from following them.

"I need your help Miss English,"

Bettie nodded. "Of course, anything,"

"I'm being blackmailed," Willow said, passing Bettie a note.

She read the note and Bettie was shocked that the blackmailer was asking for ten million pounds by tonight. That was an extreme amount of money.

As much as Bettie wanted to help the woman, she had a firm rule about extreme amounts of money. Stay out of it. The criminals that charged these sorts of rates were normally dangerous and deadly, so Bettie really wasn't going to get involved with a new baby on the way.

"I'm sorry," Bettie said, "but ten million is a lot of cash. This is a serious blackmailer. I think the police would be better suited here,"

Everyone gasped.

Willow frowned as her. "Fine then Miss English. I will give you a percent of the blackmail money,"

Bettie coughed. A hundred thousand pounds for doing this case, Bettie loved that amount. It would be amazing, that would set her up for a while in case she needed to take time off after the birth.

"Yes!" Bettie shouted.

Bettie heard everyone else breathe a sigh of relief and now she was wondering if Willow would have gotten mad if she refused.

"There's just one question I have for you Mistress Fisher," Bettie said. "I need to know what the blackmailer has on you,"

Willow Fisher looked as if she was going to hit her then Bettie watched her take a few deep breaths.

"I trust you Miss English. I am a very private woman after all, and my blackmailer has a special tape of me with a gentleman,"

Bettie shrugged. "Okay,"

Willow grabbed Bettie's arm and pulled her closer.

"Miss English, they have a sex tape of me in bed with the Local MPs son,"

Bettie smiled.

Now this was going to be interesting.

Because *after all, she was a very private woman.*

CHAPTER 6
1ˢᵗ April 2022
Canterbury, England

As Graham stood outside of the Head of Geology's Office, he really couldn't see the point of having massive cabinets lining the wide corridor filled with bright red, pink and blue rocks that were rather good to look at. But completely impractical.

Graham didn't know why the Head needed to show off his or her rock collection to all the hundreds of students that were walking, talking and laughing down the corridor.

Graham had really had to push himself into a little corner to avoid the onslaught of students that just kept coming. Judging by the time on his watch all the students would be in their classes in a moment, but he just checked his phone quickly to make sure.

His eyes lit up when he saw there was a text from Bettie, and Graham was really looking forward to seeing her tonight. He wanted to kiss and treasure her and maybe get her to talk about nursery plans for the little kid.

He felt the excitement wash over him. He really wanted to be a dad.

Willow Fisher? Graham knew that was a strange name after he read the text from Bettie, and as much as he didn't want her doing too much strange work whilst she was pregnant, he wasn't going to stop her.

If Bettie wanted to do things, be free and have fun then Graham was always going to encourage her. But he was nervous about Bettie going to some strange house in the middle of nowhere (or anywhere for that matter. He had never heard of Willow Fisher), yet at least she had Phryne with her.

Graham still wasn't sure how useful Phryne would be if anything went wrong. As Graham saw it, Phryne was all mouth about her wonderful her life was, but when it came down to it. She was next to useless about the practical things in life.

It was probably why Sean spent so much time with him and Bettie. Graham just hoped that that continued after last night. Graham had to make it right.

"Graham," a young man said behind him.

Graham turned around and smiled as he saw Sean in his normal tight jeans, very stylish loose t-shirt and designer trainers. But his eyes immediately went to Sean's new haircut where he had dyed his hair blond and had some pink pieces added.

It looked great and he really managed to pull it

off, but Graham was still getting used to it.

"Thanks for coming," Graham said slowly.

"Harry said the Head of the department always comes back from lunch at this time. And he managed to arrange an appointment for us,"

Graham smiled. He wasn't sure how Sean's boyfriend knew the Department Head considering he did computers, but he was grateful. Yet why did Sean say us?

"Us?" Graham asked, "This is police business,"

Sean frowned. "Auntie Bettie said you felt awful last night after me and mum went home. I believed her. Or was she covering for you?"

Graham didn't know what to say.

"I thought you wanted my help like you normally do. Or has the police changed you that much?" Sean said, his eyes narrow.

"Yes. I'm sorry. And I really am sorry about last night,"

Sean laughed. "You're missing the point,"

Graham cocked his head. "I thought you were mad at me for last night,"

"No," Sean said, "Auntie Bettie understood why,"

Graham really had to tell Bettie to tell him more, he didn't like getting caught out like this.

"I'm mad at what you represent. All police officers bang on about how they're there for everyone. How can people like me believe you when you keep searching and humiliating us for no reason?"

Graham just nodded and looked to the floor. He was right. Sean was absolutely right. The police was great as a whole, but it had to improve, and Graham had no idea what Sean saw in the police. But he knew that Sean was right.

The police had to get better and really serve and protect everyone.

"Excuse me please," an elderly man said.

Graham turned around and saw a rather grumpy looking man in his late sixties wearing a black suit, black shoes and a blue tie.

"Head of Geology Department?" Graham asked.

"Oh," the man said. "Are you the Police Detective and Harry's boyfriend?"

Graham nodded.

"Then please this way," the man said as he opened the office door.

Graham and Sean went inside. But Graham was hardly impressed with the musty smelling box room that only had a filing cabinet, desk and two chairs.

Graham and Sean didn't waste any time. They both quickly sat down on the chairs and frowned at the Head of Geology. Thankfully Graham saw his name on the desk, Dr Albie Peterson.

"Dr Peterson," Graham said, "thank you for meeting with me... us,"

Sean frowned.

"I was hoping you could tell us about this serial number," Graham said, passing the Doctor a scratch of paper.

"Oh yes. That is the most fine rock we have in our collection," Albie said.

"Can you tell us who had access?" Sean said.

"This is in the private section of the Collection. Only I have direct access to it, but I allow students lab time to examine them from time to time,"

Graham laughed. "Lab time?"

Albie frowned. "Detective. Geology is no joke. We conduct serious research at the university regarding how these rocks are made, studied and how they can be applied in our modern world. We could discover the next great building material,"

Graham seriously doubted that, but he didn't want to argue with a Doctor of *Geology* of all things.

Sean leant forward. "I think what the Detective meant to say was, who took out this particular rock recently? It was involved in a crime,"

"What!" Albie shouted.

Graham cocked his head. "Yes. It was thrown at my head four hours ago,"

Albie stood up and paced around his little office.

"That cannot be Detective. I finished examining the rock myself last night. I locked it away. You must be mistaken,"

"When the bruise shows up in a few days. I'll show it to you," Graham said, harshly.

Sean smiled. "So it was stolen last night, early this morning. Can you give us-"

Albie waved him silent as he got out his phone.

Graham wanted to know what he was doing, but given how protective he was of his precious rocks it might have just been easier to let him crack on.

"See Detective," Albie said, showing Graham a list of something on his phone.

It took Graham a few moments, but he realised that this was a list of people who accessed the rock collection after the good Doctor left last night and arrived this morning.

There were only three names on the list.

"There," Sean said pointing to the name at the very bottom.

"Why that one?" Graham asked.

"Because," Sean said, "The first one is a PhD student that picks up her girlfriend who works late researching rocks sometimes. The second name is a cleaner who hates names. The last one is Harry's name,"

Graham just cocked his head at that.

"What was your boyfriend doing here last night?"

Sean gave Graham a schoolboy smile. "He wasn't. He was with me,"

Graham shrugged. He knew Sean wouldn't be involved in the theft, but Harry still could have done it somehow.

Sean's smile deepened. "Graham, Harry was with me last night, all night, in bed,"

"Oh," Graham said.

With that Graham and Sean thanked Albie and left the office, Graham had to find some security footage, because if Harry wasn't involved in the crime.

Who was?

CHAPTER 7
1st April 2022
Unknown Location, Somewhere on the Outskirts of Canterbury, England

Bettie sat on a horrible hard wooden chair in a large office with ancient brown wooden walls, art and cabinets that made her feel like she was in some historical film. Even the desk in front of her was rather oversized and like it had been pulled out of world war two.

Everything in this office seemed to be ancient and definitely not from this modern age. The typewriter on the desk only proved that further.

Bettie was rather interested in the smell of it all. Instead of the office smelling awful like the living room had, it smelt rather wonderful with hints of oranges, strawberry jam and some freshly baked scones, leaving the taste of afternoon tea on her tongue.

Bettie forced herself not to gag as she imagined

clotted cream and butter being spread on the scones. And because they came from animals, she felt as if she was about to be sick.

To stop that from happening, Bettie turned her attention to the case at hand. She had left her sister to look around and speak with Mr Jones, if Bettie was lucky maybe she would find out something about him.

She doubted Phryne had that sort of mind. Bettie really hoped so.

Ten million pounds was such an extreme amount of money. She had only heard of one similar case in the private eye community and the blackmailer turned out to be some massive criminal mastermind.

But there was one fact that Bettie wanted to focus on for now. The criminal had known the victim could easily afford it, and to Bettie that meant either the criminal in this case really didn't know what Willow Fisher had. Or they were very well informed.

The door opened behind Bettie and Willow threw down a glass of water for her, and Willow sat at her desk. Bettie could smell the awfully creamy coffee, and her stomach churned.

So Bettie placed her hands on her baby bump and hoped being so close to the baby would help her feel more at ease.

"Are we alone Miss English?"

Bettie nodded, and she was starting to realise how paranoid and strange Willow was.

"I have to ask Mrs-"

"Mistress or Ms please," Willow said.

"Willow?" Bettie said.

She nodded.

"I have to ask Willow, ten million pounds. It is a lot. Have you got that sort of money?"

Willow laughed. Hard.

"Miss English, this house alone is worth twenty million and all the land included. I have ten times that sort of money. I am a world famous Self-help author you know,"

And there it was, Bettie had been wondering when the arrogance would reveal itself sooner or later.

"So why only ask for ten million?" Bettie asked.

"Miss English you are the Private Eye. You sort it out,"

Bettie nodded. She had a point, but now she knew that ten million was nothing. It made no sense to ask for so little, especially if the criminal wanted to punish her.

In Bettie's experience, blackmailers mainly wanted to punish their victims. Sure ten million would be a lot, there would be Willow's distress of knowing that someone else knew the secret and some other consequences.

But it was so strange.

Bettie leant forward. "Tell me about the… tape,"

Willow frowned. "I shall not,"

Bettie rolled her eyes. "Willow. I am trying to help you. And why didn't you call the police about the blackmail? I find that strange,"

Willow got a massive sip of her creamy coffee and Bettie rubbed her baby bump as she waited for the drink to finish. To Bettie's amazement, Willow downed the drink in one.

"I shall not call the police. I will not have them leaking my location to all the creeps in the world like your sister,"

Bettie's mouth dropped. She had heard a lot of things in her life, but she never ever expected a self-help person to moan about the people who paid her their hard-earned money to improve their lives.

Her sister might have been a lot of things, but Phryne was not a creep.

"The sex tape," Bettie said, coldly.

Willow stood up and the floor actually shook as she moved about to sit up on the desk itself. Bettie could have sworn the desk cracked a little under the weight.

"Miss English, I do trust you. But… but this is a difficult topic,"

Bettie smiled as she watched Willow debate with herself whether or not to tell her what happened. Bettie couldn't really blame her too much, the local Member of Parliament was Mrs Skylar Mason and she was wonderful. A real person who was really making a difference in the local area.

Something politicians rarely did these days.

And according to recent news reports, there was talk about Skylar becoming a Sectary of State for something, making her one of the most powerful politicians in the country if that happened.

Bettie wouldn't like to guess what would happen if it came out that her son was sleeping with a woman in her late forties.

In all honesty, Bettie couldn't have cared less but the media, the opposition parties and the general public probably would. But Bettie understood why Willow might have slept with the son, according to Sean he was hot, about the same age as him and went to the same university.

Bettie still remembered the look of shock and disappointment on Sean's face when she told him the son was perfectly straight.

"Miss English, I'll tell you,"

Bettie smiled.

"I promise myself to go outside into the real world once a year,"

Bettie just thought that was sad.

"So a few weeks ago I went to a university fundraiser and met Mrs Mason and her son. Her son made me laugh, giggle and I felt so alive. The first time since my husband died five years ago,"

Bettie was starting to feel sorry for her, but according to Sean that fundraiser was amazing for the after-party alone.

"The son asked if he could take me back. I said yes, we came back here, made out and the rest was history,"

Bettie clicked her fingers. "Did you or he ever tell

anyone? How did the sex tape get made?"

"We didn't tell anyone. We didn't do anything publicly. No one saw him come home with me. I don't know about the sex tape,"

Bettie could just nod at that. The poor woman was probably so caught up in the moment, she didn't realise someone was watching. But someone clearly had to know about it all, or else how did they know to blackmail her?

"Do you think the sex tape is real?" Bettie asked.

All the colour drained from Willow's face as she opened a drawer and threw a photo at her. Bettie gasped as she saw Willow's full front and the head of a young man rather low. As much as Bettie knew she had to keep the photo for her investigation, she really wanted to bin it.

It wasn't the most... attractive of pictures.

Bettie stood up. "Thank you. I'll start my investigation,"

Willow reached for her and Bettie cocked her head.

"Miss English. Please hurry. This cannot get out. My career has been... in tatters for a few years. I have a new course coming out and I cannot have this tape destroying it for me,"

Then Bettie realised what this was truly about and she partly wasn't surprised, Bettie had guessed it cost a lot of money to keep three people on staff and this house wouldn't be cheap to run.

"There isn't ten times the blackmail money is

there?" Bettie asked.

Willow shook her head and Bettie carefully hugged her.

As Bettie left the room, she realised she absolutely had to find out the truth. There wasn't just the reputation of a good politician, her son and a criminal going free on the line.

But a woman's livelihood too.

And Bettie couldn't allow that to suffer.

CHAPTER 8
1ˢᵗ April 2022
Canterbury, England

Graham sat down on the horribly warm desk chair in the university's security office with a large set of computer screens staring at him. He had to find out who accessed the rock collection last night, and as crazy as it sounded Graham really did believe that the drug suppliers he was after was behind the theft.

But why steal a rock?

It would have made sense if the rock was expensive and easy to sell, but from what little Graham knew about rocks where the buyers weren't on the street corners. Rocks took time to sell and from everything Graham had learnt about these drug suppliers, they were certainly not patient.

The security office smelt of strong coffee, sweat and sugary doughnuts, that made Graham really glad that beautiful Bettie wasn't here. She would have hated it and she probably would have been sick, he didn't want that for her.

But it was strange how she hadn't called him yet. They normally always chatted about lunch time and that was over an hour ago, even when they were both extremely busy they still somehow managed to call each other.

It was strange.

Graham felt his stomach tighten as he wondered if something was wrong, and if Bettie and their kid were somehow in danger.

"Love you too babe. See you tonight," Sean said as he walked into the office and put his phone away.

Graham frowned. "Um, have you heard from your mum today?"

Sean shrugged. "No. But we normally talk when I get home. We don't really talk during the day, I know she went to see Auntie Bettie and that's it,"

Graham nodded. He didn't really want to hear that, he wanted him to sound they were both okay and Bettie really had just forgotten to phone him.

Graham had to find out later where she was. As much as he hated the idea of invading her privacy like that.

"What did Harry say?" Graham asked as he clicked on the CCTV footage from last night.

"Well," Sean said with a schoolboy grin. "He lost his uni ID yesterday afternoon. He thought he lost it in the... somewhere where we were making out,"

Graham just smiled. Sean and Harry were almost as bad as him and Bettie, he didn't want anyone to know the places they made out in.

"But it turned out the most logical place for him to lose it was in his Law lecture at 3 pm," Sean said.

Graham nodded as he found the footage of the rock collection from last night. He started to play it and fast-forwarded.

"Why did he have access to the rock collection?" Graham asked.

Sean shrugged. "This is a uni. Everyone's pass allows them into different sections, but the rock one is one of the few you need a special pass to,"

Graham slowed down the footage as he saw the cleaner and another enter, do their business and leave.

"But I think Harry helps out at the rock collection or he did at one time. I think he was helping update the collection's computer records,"

Graham smiled at that. That was plain embarrassing when the university had to rely on students to do their IT work for them.

Graham double-checked the time when Harry's ID was apparently used and he slowed down the footage as someone entered the collection.

It was clearly a man entering the long corridor then he took out the ID, scanned it and went into the collection. Graham stopped the footage. The footage was definitely not the best he had ever seen. He could barely make out much more than the criminal's gender.

"He's fit," Sean muttered.

Graham turned and looked at him. "You have a

boyfriend,"

Sean smiled. "And you're dating my Auntie. I saw you eyeing up that older student on the way here,"

Graham just focused on the footage, sometimes these young people were too observant for their own good.

"Actually," Sean said, leaning over Graham. "Can you blow that up for me please?"

Graham didn't want to get into the complex nature about how photos couldn't be blown up like in the movies, but he could zoom in.

"I think I know who that is," Sean said.

"How! There is no way you could get anything from that photo," Graham said, rather annoyed.

Sean folded his arms. "Oh why, because of your superior training?"

Graham nodded fiercely. "Yes!"

Sean playfully hit Graham over the head. "That's Arlo Mason,"

Graham shrugged. He had no clue who that guy was but judging by the massive smile on Sean's face he clearly knew the man.

"You know," Sean said, "the son of the Politician Skylar Mason,"

"Oh!" Graham shouted.

That really changes things now. Not only because Sean was implicating a major politician's son was involved, making it next to impossible to interview him, but because Sean's ID was useless in a court of law.

They needed proof.

"How do you know that's him?" Graham asked, hoping for some useable proof to interview Arlo.

Sean just smiled. "We have a class together and he's… he has the looks and body and smile of a model. I know what he looks like,"

As much as Graham wanted to tell him off for staring at another person, he couldn't do that. He was sure if a supermodel or female model walked past him, Graham would have to look and stare.

And he doubted Bettie would be any different. All that mattered was Graham only loved Bettie, and he knew Sean only loved Harry.

Graham stood up and started to leave the security office.

"Where we going?" Sean asked.

"We need to get some prints and see Arlo,"

"Yes!" Sean said involuntarily.

Graham just laughed. He knew that Sean was going to be very helpful in collecting these prints.

But he was felt concerned about Bettie.

He just hoped she was okay.

CHAPTER 9
1ˢᵗ April 2022

Unknown Location, Somewhere on the Outskirts of Canterbury, England

Bettie really couldn't understand why she wasn't allowed her phone and couldn't leave, she was basically trapped. All Bettie had wanted was to go back to the office quickly to do a bit of research on the son and maybe ask Sean a few questions.

But that apparently wasn't allowed, all because Bettie might tell people where Willow Fisher lived. Bettie couldn't care less about this arrogant and probably pompous self-help person. No one probably cared where she lived, but if her sister was anything to go by, maybe Willow was right to keep her location secret.

Bettie stood in the doorway of Willow's bedroom that was rather wonderful considering the rest of the house. Bettie liked the massive Queen size bed in the middle of the room with its black silk sheets, massive pillows and two bedside cabinets.

What Bettie didn't like where all the portraits hanging on the white walls. If Bettie and Graham had tried to do it here, Bettie would have to stop. Even now she felt as if they were all watching her.

It didn't help Bettie felt any better when the faces on the portraits were done so perfectly and life-like. Bettie wondered when the people were going to climb through them, but she had to focus.

The smell of the staff's roast dinner and massive lunch made Bettie gag a few times as the wonderful hints of crispy potatoes, juicy, succulent meat and roasted vegetables filled the air. Bettie had to shut the bedroom door as she went inside.

Bettie had no idea where Phryne went too, but she was enjoying the quiet. Bettie just hoped her sister didn't eat their lunch and come to her stinking of meat and everything. Phryne still didn't believe Bettie that ever since her pregnancy animal products turned her stomach.

"Where would I take a dodgy photo?" Bettie asked to herself as she rubbed her baby bump.

The bedroom was large enough to hide cameras in a range of places, but the photo was the key. Before Bettie only focused on Willow's body and the young man, but now she needed to focus on it as a Private Eye.

There weren't too many markers in the background of the photo except the white walls, golden frames and the silk sheets. None of which helped Bettie as they only proved the photo could have been taken from anywhere in the bedroom.

Yet the lighting was interesting.

Bettie looked up and saw that the central chandelier that hung down from the ceiling over the bed (another reason why Bettie could never sleep here) was only decorative. No light came from it.

Instead all the light seemed to be coming from the four spotlights in the corners of the bedroom that focused on the bed. Bettie really wasn't keen on that, it was what she expected from adult content creators, not a self-help person.

Bettie checked each light and smiled when she discovered only three of the lights worked. That was brilliant because it meant that the lighting would be off in the room with there being a much darker area in the photo.

Hopefully.

The bedroom door opened releasing a massive wave of crispy roast meat smell and Phryne walked in a massive plate of roast dinner for Bettie.

Bettie gagged, coughed and huffed as Phryne passed her the plate.

Bettie vomited.

All over the plate and Phryne.

Phryne ran out.

Bettie finished vomiting and went over to the bedroom to catch her breath. She rubbed her baby bump and felt the little one kick a few times.

That really made her smile.

Bettie had to admit the bedroom was really comfortable and the silk sheets made her feel so special and rich for a few seconds. She certainly wouldn't mind doing adult stuff on these sheets.

But the lighting was still strange and Bettie realised she had seen the dark patch on the bed before. Bettie got out the photo and saw in the top left-hand corner it was almost completely dark.

Bettie turned on the bed and positioned herself so her right was facing the broken light and she found it. Right in front of her was a massive portrait of some military general riding a black horse.

It had to be where the photo was taken but Bettie wasn't sure how it could have been taken there.

Bettie went over to the photo and ran her fingers over its cold surface to try and find a camera or something.

The door opened and Bettie heard the sloshing of water as Phryne came in with a bucket and mop.

"You weren't kidding about that vegan thing were you?" Phryne said.

"Believe me, my body doesn't like animal products," Bettie said firmly.

"I thought you were lying for the past four months,"

Bettie didn't even respond to that. She was more stunned her own sister thought she would lie to her.

"What are you doing Bettie? I know your hobby is strange but must you touch up a canvas?"

Bettie really wanted to throw something at her.

"I'm trying to look for a camera," Bettie said.

Phryne huffed. "Seriously? The stuff you and your hobbyists come up with. You are just stupid if you ask me,"

Bettie heard Phryne gasp as soon as she said it but the damage was done. Bettie was furious that her damn sister would call her such a thing, Bettie's work mattered to a lot of good people, and if Phryne couldn't see that then Bettie would rather have her out of her life.

Completely.

"Bet I'm-"

Bettie pointed a finger at Phryne. "Save it,"

Bettie went back to the canvas and smiled as she felt a little lump on the horse's nose. So she picked it, and it turned out someone had added extra paint to this section and once Bettie removed it, she really smiled.

A very small camera fell onto the floor, Bettie picked it up and grinned as she saw a serial number on the back.

"Am I still stupid?" Bettie asked, showing Phryne the camera.

Phryne just left the room without taking it back.

And that killed Bettie.

CHAPTER 10
1st April 2022
Canterbury, England

Graham really wasn't sure about sending Sean in to do this, but as he leant on the glass railings overlooking the canteen area which had tens upon tens of tables, noisy students and cafes lining the area. Graham had to admit he really did not fit in here.

During his own university days that were rather hazy, Graham had never had this much choice about where to eat, drink and study. He was definitely glad Sean had more choice, but this all felt too exposed.

At least the air smelt wonderfully of sweet cakes, pastries and rich sweet hot chocolate that all combined to make a heavenly taste form on his tongue. Graham was having to remember to pick some stuff before he went home, ever since Bettie had fallen pregnant he had had to limit his non-vegan treats.

Graham focused on Sean's blond hair with

tasteful pink mixed in as he went into the canteen area and looked for Arlo. As he watched Sean find Arlo and look at him for a moment, Graham couldn't help but feel bad for him.

Other police officers that Graham considered "friends" would never have allowed him to send in Sean. They would have stupidly been afraid of him blowing the operation all because he was clearly gay with his slightly pink hair.

Graham didn't understand other officers in fairness, the vast majority of them were great. It was just the old fashioned officers that ruined it for the rest of them. Graham really wanted that to change, and he was even going to risk his reputation slightly by spelling out Sean's contribution in his case report.

Graham focused on Arlo as Sean started talking to him. He understood why Sean thought he was attractive, Arlo's hair was perfectly cut and managed and styled like most models and it framed his smooth handsome face perfectly. And Graham was hardly surprised to see Arlo had perfectly strong cheekbones and judging by his too-tight t-shirt he had the physique of a Greek god.

Graham was starting to feel slightly inadequate.

"Graham?" someone said behind him.

Graham turned around and his mouth opened when he saw a female officer. He couldn't remember the name off the top of his head, but he knew he had seen the woman about the police station.

This new officer wore a long white dress, high

heels and her long blond hair was perfectly cut.

"Hi what are you doing here?" Graham asked.

"I was volunteering with the hair department. What are doing here?"

Graham was about to reveal his operation (which was so overdramatic) but he knew from past experience never to reveal his full hand to his fellow officers.

"Just waiting for my niece to get out of class," Graham said, carefully watching Arlo and Sean.

Thankfully they were both having a massive conversation.

"Mine if I wait with you. I waiting for my daughter to pick me up,"

"Sure," Graham said, feeling his stomach tighten as he remembered her name.

Officer Serenity Simpson was a very good friend of the police officer who searched that schoolboy for no good reason. Graham really hoped she didn't see Sean.

But she did.

"Ha. Just look at that man down there with his blond and pink hair. Ha,"

Graham stayed silent.

"I mean come on, Graham. If that happened when we were at school we would have beaten the kid up or at least the boys would. It's all just character building,"

Graham wanted to stay silent, but wasn't that half the problem with the police? Didn't all the police officers say silent instead of challenging behaviour?

Graham always defended women from the sexism they experience, so why didn't he stand up for his own nephew?

As much as Graham wanted things to change in the police, he realised that he needed to start changing as a result. If Sean was completely right last night, he was just part of the problem and not the solution.

"I don't know," Graham said, "if it makes him happy. Shouldn't he be allowed to express himself?"

Serenity laughed. "Oh yeah. Express himself to the little girl he always was. It's pathetic. You have to agree, all the police officers think that,"

"This officer does not!" Graham shouted as loud as he could.

The entire canteen below fell silent.

"What is wrong with you?" Serenity shouted.

"If people want to be gay, express themselves and do whatever that is their business. We are the police! We defend everyone no matter what we think personally!" Graham shouted.

Serenity laughed at him. "Careful Graham people might think you're one of them soon!"

Then she just walked away.

Graham's eyes narrowed on that idiot officer and he slowly turned back to focus on the canteen.

Only everyone was staring at him, Arlo was storming off but there was one thing that made Graham smile and know he had done the right thing.

Sean was staring at him with a massive smile.

But most important Sean was carefully holding a coffee mug in his hand.

At last Graham had his prints.

A VERY PRIVATE WOMAN

CHAPTER 11
1st April 2022

Unknown Location, Somewhere On the Outskirts of Canterbury, England

"What do you mean I can't leave?" Bettie said.

She was furious as she stood in the bedroom with the Queen size bed, portraits on the walls and chandelier hanging overhead. This was flat out ridiculous, Bettie was trying to help them and they wouldn't let her leave.

She needed to escape, go back to the office and try and run the serial number of the camera she had just found to prove why the sex tape had been taken on this very camera. Then she needed to find out if this model of secret camera transmitted the footage or did someone need to collect it and download the footage.

Bettie just stared at Willow Fisher and Mr Jones as they barred her from leaving. Of course Phryne was nowhere to be seen and quite frankly Bettie didn't care. If her sister wanted to believe she was stupid for being a Private Eye, helping people and solving crimes then Bettie didn't want her in her life anymore.

Bettie forced herself not to gag, cough or vomit as she started to smell hints of the roast dinner lunch on Willow and Mr Jones. But Bettie wouldn't mind vomiting on them after their outrageous behaviour.

"Listen to me," Bettie said, "I need to go and run this serial number on the camera. I have to help you stop this blackmailer,"

Willow laughed. "I'm sorry. But Mr Jones was talking with your sister and we learnt tons about you. It seems like you are not the Private Eye everyone thinks you are,"

Bettie's hands formed fists. She hated her sister. How dare she spread lies about Bettie. Not respecting her career choice, Bettie could and would live with, but actively trying to discredit her. That was a new low.

"It seems like you tend to make sure wild theories to impress your clients and get their money," Mr Jones said, who was oddly a less formal now.

In fact both of them were and that was strange. Earlier these people had been so formal, stuck up and pompous. But they had changed now, probably because they didn't think Bettie was useful.

Bettie was going to prove them wrong.

"My sister lies," Bettie said firmly.

Mr Jones laughed. "Miss English, your sister said you said say that. In fact, we have decided to take up your sister's offers of legal representation. She has gotten her phone back and is now connecting to our printers so we can sign the legal paperwork,"

Bettie frowned. "What legal paperwork?"

Willow smiled. "Miss English, the legal paperwork making it illegal for you to discuss anything about today. Including my name, the location of my property and anything you have seen,"

Bettie laughed. This was ridiculous.

"And if you continue to investigate and make up more lies. Then we will sue you, Miss English," Mr Jones said.

"What about my money?" Bettie asked.

In all fairness, with a kid on the way that was what she was more concerned with.

Willow grinned. "What money? Once you sign the legal paperwork, you will not be able to discuss money whatsoever. Including any money I may or may not have promised,"

Bettie gasped and fell onto the bed. This was one of the worse cases she had ever been involved in. This was completely outrageous, and Bettie didn't doubt for a second her sister suggested the thing about the money.

But what Bettie was stunned about was the massive 180 these two people had done in the past few hours. A few hours ago Bettie was the most important person to them, now she was the enemy it seemed

"Why?" Bettie asked.

"Because your sister wants you to stop lying, creating crazy conspiracy theories and get a real job," Mr Jones said.

Not exactly what Bettie wanted to know, but that

was useful for later she hoped.

"No," Bettie said, "Why the change? It isn't because you think I'm lying. What does the blackmailer know?"

Both Willow and Mr Jones frowned and took a few steps back.

"Willow please. I can help!" Bettie shouted.

Willow and Mr Jones each gave a nervous laugh and just shook their heads and slowly started to walk out of the room.

"See Mr Jones," Willow said. "She is simply creating more lies,"

"I see, I see Mistress,"

Then they both stopped.

"Miss English," Mr Jones said, "Where's the camera you found?"

Bettie shook her head. That was the last thing she was going to tell these people. If there was a sex tape on the camera, then Bettie was seriously considering using it, even if she had to fade out the face of Arlo Mason.

"Lost it," Bettie said smiling.

Willow Fisher looked like she was about to slap Bettie but her and Mr Jones ran out of the room.

Shut the door.

And locked Bettie in.

CHAPTER 12
1ˢᵗ April 2022
Canterbury, England

As Graham stood in the long blue corridor of the Crime scene section of the police department outside two silver doors waiting for Zoey to come out with the results from the fingerprints, he couldn't deny he was worried.

This was extremely unlike Bettie to just go dark for this long. Graham was never going to ask her to keep him informed of every single movement, he was far from that sort of boyfriend. But he was worried.

As long as Graham could remember Bettie had never been missing for this long, and even as Graham tried to call her, it kept going to answer phone.

It was strange.

Graham had even tried to call Phryne twenty times, and still she wasn't answering too. If Graham didn't already know how anal Phryne was keeping her phone on in case there was an important client, he wouldn't have been worried. But now he was extremely worried.

Something had to be wrong.

The smell of lemons, harsh chemicals and almonds filled the air as doors opened and forensic people went into other rooms, Graham couldn't deny he was extremely tempted to ask Zoey to try and find where Bettie's phone was.

Graham wished he had kept Sean with him now, but apparently Sean had a class so he had to go. Graham really wanted him in case Phryne was blocking his calls, but he doubted even she would block on her own son. Granted he wouldn't put it past her.

"Detective Adams," a deep manly voice said.

Graham turned around and rolled his eyes as a large, overweight man walked towards him wearing a very official looking police uniform. Graham knew it was the Captain of this particular police station, and he was meant to be some hot shot detective from back in the day. But Graham didn't think he was very good.

He was practically useless nowadays. As far as Graham was concerned he was nothing more than a desk jockey using his power to benefit him and his gang and not the people they served and protected.

Graham smiled as it meant perfect sense that Officer Serenity would go there first. That's the only reason this Captain would come to see him.

"Captain Aiden Yates," Graham said, smiling, "it is an honour,"

"It is far from an honour to meet you," Aiden

said.

Graham was a bit taken back by the comment. No one had ever been that rude to him before.

"Detective Adams, I am here due to a concerning report of you abusing another officer,"

Graham forced himself not to smile. He was looking forward to seeing what lies Serenity had told him.

"I did no such thing," Graham said.

"Apparently, you are being extremely homophobic and abusive towards the people we serve. I would like to remind you the police protect everyone,"

Graham's mouth dropped. He had to give Serenity credit, she did know how to be original with her rumours. Graham was not expecting her to take this direction.

"Sir, I am not a homophobe. My own nephew is gay"

Aiden laughed. "That only confirms her story even more. She said you were taking out your rage at him towards the other gay students at the university. This is unacceptable,"

"She is lying!" Graham shouted.

Aiden shook his head. "Detective, after the incident with you and that other officer humiliating that gay school kid. I am afraid I believe her and I am suspending you til further notice,"

Graham really wished his mouth could drop even further. This was ridiculous. But thankfully Graham knew he still had a few friends in high places, and most of all, Graham had to find Bettie.

The drug case would probably be passed over to another officer, but Graham couldn't stop investigating just yet. He didn't know why, but he couldn't help but feel like Bettie's disappearance was involved in.

And Graham was going to protect, love and find Bettie no matter what policing rules he broke.

He just needed to buy himself time.

"Of course Sir," Graham said, bowing his head.

Aiden smiled. "Very good Detective. I want you gone from the building in ten minutes and because you have gone easily, you shall be paid,"

"Thank you Sir," Graham said, as he watched the idiot Aiden walk away.

The two silver doors opened and Zoey popped out in her white lab coat.

"You aren't going anywhere are you?" she asked.

"You heard that?" Graham asked.

"Of course, and technically I shouldn't tell you this, but I didn't know you were suspended, cough, cough," Zoey said with a suspicious smile.

Graham smiled too. He knew he liked her for a reason.

"The fingerprints you got from Mr Arlo were not a match for the fingerprints on the rock. But it turned out your nephew got a DNA sample too. Turned out Arlo had very sweaty hands when he was talking to Sean. That got me a DNA match on the rock. I managed to recover touch DNA on it,"

Graham cocked his head. "So Arlo did steal the rock,"

"Yes, what probably happened was he was wearing gloves when he actually stole it. But he handled the gloves very well beforehand, transferring DNA onto the glove material. I do love my new toys!"

Graham nodded. He did too. Then he looked to the floor, he had to know about Bettie.

"What's wrong Graham?" Zoey asked.

"I need a favour," Graham said.

"Like where Bettie is?" Zoey asked.

Graham's mouth dropped. There was no way she could have known about that situation.

"Yes, but how?" Graham asked, shocked.

Zoey smiled. "Turned out our Bettie is a very clever woman. It seems that she installed a security protocol on her phone when you both started dating,"

Graham nodded slowly.

"The Protocol means if her phone turns off and isn't turned back on in six hours, the service she uses a text message to Sean,"

"Who sent it to you?" Graham asked.

"Yep, he knows my brother he works at the university, so he got my number from him. And I managed to get a rough location on her phone,"

Graham laughed. This was the best work for ages, he loved how Zoey would ping a phone's last location by looking at the phone towers it pinged off.

"And even better. There's only one structure in the area and there are people inside," Zoey said.

Graham hugged her and kissed her forehead. "Thank you!"

Graham quickly walked down the corridor.

He had to get out of the building.

And save the woman he loved.

Cop or not.

He was going to do that.

CHAPTER 13
1st April 2022
Unknown Location, Somewhere On The Outskirts of Canterbury, England

Bettie raised her fists to smash on the massive wooden door, but she lowered them. The door might have been ancient but it was strong. Smashing it would be simply useless and in case things did keep getting worse then Bettie knew she had to keep up her strength.

Not only for herself but the baby too.

As Bettie took a few steps away from the wooden door, she focused on the massive Queen size bed with its black silk sheets, and the horrible art on the walls and the chandelier hanging over the bed. There was still something flat out wrong here.

The little camera she had found was your normal spyware that Bettie knew from experience that anyone could and would easily order it. But when Bettie got out the little camera and looked at it, she noticed it was very much wireless.

Yet if experience had taught her anything, it was these cameras have very small range when it comes to someone being able to download the footage.

That made perfect sense.

Especially because it was clear the blackmailer had contacted them again. That was the only explanation Bettie could come up with to why Mistress Fisher and Mr Jones had changed their tunes so much. It was so strange.

What was even stranger was, what could the blackmailer possibly have on them that would make them give up their hopes on Bettie? Willow Fisher said it herself that she loved Bettie and knew she was the best.

So it made even less sense for Mistress Fisher to change her tune.

Unless whatever Phryne had said had really affected what Willow Fisher thought of her. But even that made no real sense, Bettie and Phryne had always had their differences and as much as Bettie hated her sister for forcing her to want to pursue a real job.

Phryne would hate actively trying to sabotage her.

Something else had to be going on.

And Phryne only really started to change after the conversation with Mr Jones, and Bettie went off to talk with Willow Fisher.

Bettie felt the colour draining from her face as she realised that her sister was... being blackmailed or something too. It explained why Phryne was acting like an idiot and purposefully trying to discourage Bettie.

It even made sense why Mr Jones and Willow Fisher had tried to convince Bettie of her sister's lies. Because they were lying to her.

Bettie focused on the little camera again and then took out the photo Willow had given her that was meant to prove the sex tape was real. Bettie realised that the little spyware camera was just that.

A camera. One that could only take photos, not videos.

Bettie must have been so annoyed earlier that she didn't realise it sooner. Both Bettie and Graham had spoken about this model of camera before, they both laughed about how pathetic it was practically.

Then Bettie's eyes narrowed on the photo itself. It was too perfect.

Normally when Bettie had had to look at explicit photos before, they were always something rather rushed, chaotic or plain amateur about them. But this particular photo was expertly done, and if Bettie hadn't been distracted earlier with the case, she might have thought it was a professional shot.

It was almost like Willow Fisher had been on the bed whilst someone positioned the camera before the university fundraiser.

That was the only logical explanation.

But where was Phryne?

Bettie rushed over to the door. She had to

protect her sister.

"Phryne!" Bettie shouted. "Get out!"

Nothing.

"Phryne! Get out!"

Still nothing.

"Phryne! Get out!"

Then Bettie smiled as she heard footsteps coming up to the door.

The door unlocked. Bettie could a few steps back.

Mrs Lewis walked in with a rolling pin. Bettie hated her little maid outfit that did nothing for her oversized figure.

Bettie covered her baby bump.

"You tart bitch!" Mrs Lewis shouted. "I ain't gonna hurt us,"

Bettie still didn't move. She wasn't taking any chances.

"Now you listen here bitch!" Mrs Lewis shouted. "You ain't going anywhere. That dumb as a post sister of yours is not going anywhere,"

A frying pan smashed down.

Smashing onto Mrs Lewis.

Something cracked.

Mrs Lewis collapsed to the ground.

Bettie grabbed the rolling pin. Pointing it at the door.

Mr Harman walked in his black tracksuit, shoes and a massive smile on his face.

"You okay Miss English?" he said.

Bettie was about to answer when she noticed how different he sounded. He definitely wasn't the same man she met earlier.

"Who are you?" Bettie asked pointing the rolling pin at his head.

An arm wrapped round Mr Harman's throat.

Holding him in a headlock.

"You okay Bet?" Phryne asked.

Bettie's mouth dropped as she stared at the massive black eye and swollen jaw of her sister.

"Should I be asking you that question?" Bettie asked.

Phryne tightened her headlock. "My sis asked you a question,"

"Friend of your boyfriends. Officer Caleb Young," he said.

Bettie smiled. She remembered the man, and she remembered that was the name of the officer that humiliated that gay school kid.

Bettie smashed the rolling pin over his head.

"Ouch!"

"That's for that school kid," Bettie said.

Phryne tightened her headlock and choked him til he passed out. He dropped to the ground.

"Seriously?" Bettie said.

"Come on Bet. We need to go. They're going after Sean and Graham. I didn't want to abuse you anymore," Phryne said.

Bettie nodded.

They both rushed out the door.

They had to escape.
They had to find Graham.
They had to save them both.
And Bettie had to find out the truth.
Something very wrong was going on here.
Something dangerously wrong.

CHAPTER 14
1st April 2022

2 Miles Outside Canterbury, England

Graham hated the disgusting Tudor-style house with its stupid white walls, gravel drive and silly large door that he walked straight towards.

The air smelt awful with hints of crispy potatoes, succulent meat and roasted vegetables. Graham hated to imagine what torture Bettie was going through.

He had to get in there.

Graham might not have been a cop now, but he was going to do anything to save the woman he loved. He had to find a way inside.

When he got to the large wooden door, Graham raised his fist to knock. But if there were bad guys or criminals in there, he knew he couldn't just knock. The last thing he wanted was to alarm them and even make them attack Bettie.

He was going to have to break in.

And if anyone questioned him later on, Graham

would just say he heard screaming inside, and it wasn't exactly like Bettie and Phryne were going to call him a liar.

Graham took a few steps back.

He ran at the door.

The door opened.

Bettie came out.

Phryne walked her to one side.

Graham tackled Phryne to the ground.

Graham's head whacked into hers.

"Get off me you bastard!" Phryne shouted in pain.

Graham quickly got off her.

He covered his mouth with his hands the moment he saw Phryne's swollen jaw and black eye.

She was rocking herself on the floor in crippling pain.

Graham looked at Bettie with her amazing hair, sexy body and those stunning eyes. Graham kissed her. Hard.

"Took you long enough," Bettie said with a smile.

Graham cocked his head. "I didn't know you needed rescuing,"

The sound of two people walking down the stairs made Graham look at that stupid homophobic officer Caleb Young and a woman in a maid's outfit.

He didn't even want to know about them.

"Bettie English," Young said, "you are under arrest for assaulting an officer,"

Graham frowned. He might have stood by Young humiliating a gay schoolboy. But this ended now!

Graham flew over to him.

Punched him in the head.

Then the woman in the maid outfit fainted.

"That should buy us some time," Graham said.

"Summary!" Bettie shouted, going out the front door.

Damn, Graham loved Bettie.

"Drug crimes. Arlo Mason involved. I'm suspended. Summary?" Graham said.

Bettie kept walking towards Graham's car, Phryne followed them.

"Your cases are connected. Massive deception here. We need to save Sean,"

Graham didn't need to hear anymore.

He had to protect Sean.

He had to stop the criminals.

He had to find out what the hell was going on here.

But at least he was doing it with the woman he loved.

CHAPTER 15
1ˢᵗ April 2022
Canterbury, England

Bettie stormed into the university canteen.

She flat out hated the rows upon rows of little metal tables. They were so annoying. She hated the loud talking, laughing and joking of students.

Bettie had to find Sean.

Bettie looked at all the different cafes, vending machines and restaurants that lined the canteen walls. He wasn't there. Harry said he would be here. There was nowhere else for him to be.

Sean wasn't even picking up his damn phone. He could be dead all for Bettie knew. She couldn't let anything happen to him, especially after Bettie had dropped Phryne off at the hospital.

Bettie's eyes narrowed on all the students. She had to see Sean's blond and pink hair. She shouldn't be able to miss it.

Glass smashed.

Bettie spun around.

Students went silent.

She couldn't see anything.

More glass smashed.

It was coming ahead of her.

Bettie flew forward.

Towards the students.

More glass smashed.

"Sean!" Bettie shouted.

Bettie threw other students to the ground.

But after Bettie threw some students to the ground and they moaned, all she saw were some dropped glasses where some students had bumped into each other as they went to get their evening meals.

All the students gave Bettie strange looks as if she was somehow crazy, they quickly walked away.

"Auntie?" Sean said.

Bettie spun around and hugged him tight.

The other students just shook their heads and muttered to each other and walked away.

"I take it there's a reason you're killing my street cred," Sean said.

Bettie was about to say something when she realised that Sean was never in danger. She didn't doubt what Phryne heard, but it didn't fit with how Willow Fisher behaved.

Everything from the beginning had been a misdirection and deception. So why would an attack on Graham and Sean be any different?

Bettie needed to regroup with her family and see what was actually going on.

Bettie looked at Sean. "Want to solve a crime tonight?"

Sean smiled. "Why not?"

Bettie and Sean walked out of the canteen, and Bettie realised there were so many questions on her mind and so few answers.

But Bettie also needed to make another phone call.

She needed to see if a certain politician would pay them a visit.

CHAPTER 16
1st April 2022
Canterbury, England

Sitting on one of Bettie's beanbags in her office around her wooden desk that was covered in folders and her laptop, Graham was extremely relieved that Sean was okay. He didn't know what he would have done if anything had happened to him.

Thankfully Bettie and him had explained everything to each other. Graham was outraged that Willow Fisher and Mr Jones had threatened to kill Sean and Bettie if Phryne didn't help them with the "Bettie Problem".

But the problem was there were too many questions that didn't have answers. And that was why sexy Bettie had called them all together, and Graham was really looking forward to getting some answers.

The utterly wonderful smell of vegan (and baby friendly) Chinese food filled the office as Sean came through the door with two large bags. Graham got up and helped him put the bags on Bettie's desk and they both passed out the food to the others.

"How's mum?" Sean asked.

Graham shook his head. He hated the fact he'd had to take Phryne to the hospital for stitches and pain meds.

"She'll be out tomorrow thankfully," he said.

Sean nodded. He was still clearly concerned. Graham wished his kid would be that concerned in a few decades time.

Graham blew Bettie a few kisses as she sat in her desk chair using her baby bump as a little tray for her food. He loved it when she did that, she looked adorable.

Graham grabbed a box of vegan chicken curry and noodles (he guessed the noodles made it Chinese) and pointed his chopsticks at Bettie.

"So Fisher hires you and brings you to her private home, why?" Graham asked.

Bettie finished a mouthful. "I suspect it's because she wanted a reputable Private Eye to cover her if anything went wrong,"

Graham nodded. It made sense.

He tasted some of the chicken curry and his mouth exploded with the amazing tastes of the creamy sauce, amazingly flavoured (vegan) chicken and wonderful spices.

"But why," Sean said, "seduce a politician's son? I mean he's hot as hell, but why?"

Graham and Bettie just smiled at that, and in

Bettie's sexy grin, he knew that she had thought similar about other people in the past. Graham was relieved a little to know he wasn't the only one.

"Because," Bettie said, "this rock's worth tens of thousands of pounds,"

Graham pointed his chopstick at Bettie. "What about this course deal or something? Would that cover the costs of the household and make her millions?"

Bettie looked at Sean and Graham and shrugged. "Sean, did mum ever say what… service, website, whatever Willow used?"

Sean looked to the floor then looked up again.

"Yeah Auntie. Some place called New Horizon Publishing Limited,"

Graham watched Bettie open her laptop and look something up. She shook her head.

"Another deception," she said. "The company closed three months ago due to… theft,"

Graham finished another amazing mouthful. "Yes I remember that case. I was floating in that department at the time. New Horizons was publishing a new geology book at the time and do a lot of geology courses,"

Bettie grinned and Graham couldn't blame her. He had no idea why a publishing company would think a geology book and courses would make them money.

"Then the company was broken into," Graham said, "and the camera equipment and the hard drives for the courses were stolen. Later found burnt,"

"Who did it?" Sean asked.

Graham shook his head. He actually couldn't remember. The cops could have found the criminals, but he doubted it. He was interested in the case at the time, Graham would have liked to think he would have remembered that sort of detail.

"They never found them," Graham said.

"So what if Fisher was involved?" Bettie said.

Graham just shook his hands. "Wait, how does this connect to today? So Willow's publishing company closes because of a theft. Do we think she would actually steal from the company making her millions?"

Sean slurped some of his dinner. "Sorry. But how do we know the company was making her millions?"

Graham nodded at Bettie. He had to admit Sean was useful. He never would have considered that question.

Graham got up and walked over to Bettie. It didn't take them long to realise that the website didn't mention Willow whatsoever. She wasn't even listed on the product pages.

"So the company drops her," Bettie said, "and she wants revenge?"

Graham shook his head. "No. She was probably dropped for the geology products. Willow hated to prove the company wrong,"

Sean nodded. "She destroys the products hoping New Horizons would take her back,"

"But we shall not," someone said at the door.

Graham and Bettie looked up. Graham smiled as a tall elegant woman in a tight business suit walked in. Her high heels pounded into the floor and Graham instantly recognised her as Skylar Mason.

"Mrs Mason," Graham said, bowing his head, "thank you for coming. This is-"

Skylar waved him silent. "Forgive me Detective. I know who you are and I am concerned. My son confessed everything to me after your nephew spoke to him,"

Graham shook his head and smiled as Sean blushed.

Bettie stood up. "You know about New Horizons?"

Skylar went over to the door and closed it firmly.

"I am an investor, and I have some unofficial powers on the board of directors. I was the one who encouraged the board to drop Miss Fisher,"

Graham and Bettie winked at each other. It was all starting to make sense now.

"Did you know it was Willow that broke into your company?" Graham asked.

"Of course and we told the officers everything. Willow Fisher was a very demanding, high maintenance and a very private woman so promotion was starting to become a nightmare. As well as she was costing the company far more than she was making us," Skylar said.

Graham wasn't impressed. Those officers should

have investigated a lot harder and it shouldn't have been that hard to find links between the theft and Willow Fisher.

"I presume," Skylar said, "Willow seduced my son on purpose that night. I... cannot always condone my son in his sexual activities, but I do not doubt for a second Willow bumped into my son on purpose that night,"

Graham nodded. He was not going to disagree, but the blackmail was extreme.

"Then she bought your son," Bettie said, "back to her place for sex. She took some photos and blackmailed your son into stealing the rock from the collection. Assuming to make a bit more money from the geology products that costed her, her livelihood apparently,"

"Exactly," Graham and Skylar said.

Bettie cocked her head and looked at Graham. "Then how did the rock end up in the hands of drug suppliers?"

Graham opened his mouth and hoped some kind of answer popped out of his mouth. Nothing did.

Sean finished off his food and binned the container.

"Another question is where are Willow now?" Sean said.

Graham waved his chopsticks about. "Skylar, who investigated the theft?"

Graham felt his stomach tighten as he already knew the answer.

"I only ever spoke to two people. An Officer Sarah… no Serenity Simpson and a detective… Harman… no. Caleb Young,"

Graham just shook his head.

Something major was going on here.

He just didn't know everything yet.

But if cops were dirty and secret criminals.

Then that terrified Graham more than he ever wanted to admit.

CHAPTER 17
2nd April 2022
Rochester, England

After a wonderful night's rest, Bettie and Graham quickly drove to the historical City of Rochester with its old cobblestone high street, little shops and plenty of Victorian charm.

Bettie stared at Caleb Young who's face was covered in bandages and Serenity Simpson who were walking along the high street arm in arm and smiling with each other. Bettie hated them both.

They were somehow involved and Bettie had to find out how.

"Graham!" Caleb shouted then looked in crippling pain as Bettie and Graham stopped in front of them.

"You are suspended. You homophobic jerk," Serenity said.

Bettie could actually understand these two being together. They were both awful, homophobic and pathological liars it seemed. Bettie had to deal with them at some point.

"I was only suspended because of your lies," Graham said.

Bettie subtly turned on the recording app on her phone just in case it was useful.

"Why didn't you investigate Willow Fisher three months ago?" Bettie asked.

Caleb laughed. "Seriously? Three months ago. I don't know what I was-"

Bettie waved him silent. "The theft case at New Horizons Publishing. You investigated. The staff told you who did it, you did nothing. Why?"

Serenity just shook her head at Bettie. "You Amateur Sleuths are all the same,"

Bettie wanted to smash her lights out. She was not an Amateur Sleuth. She had trained for months, if not years before she became a licensed Private Eye, and she was damn good too.

"We didn't investigate her because she...," Caleb trailed off and looked at his idiot of a girlfriend.

"She paid us good money to stay quiet. And in case you think that makes us corrupt, we will plead that we were tricking her. Then we sent in-"

Bettie waved her silent. She could really guess that they would plead something stupid like they were making the criminal drop her guard so Caleb could go undercover as Mr Harman to catch the criminal.

But that couldn't be the truth.

If that was true then it wouldn't make sense for

Willow Fisher to hire someone she knew to be a cop. Especially for her plan to work, after all it was Caleb who had tried to free Bettie when she was captured.

Or did he?

Bettie wasn't sure now. In fact, she only really escaped when Phryne had intervened, and the second Caleb had the chance he tried to arrest Bettie for assaulting him. He shouldn't have done that.

"How long have you been on the take?" Bettie asked.

Caleb took a few steps back.

"You didn't come to free me when I was trapped. I suspect you were coming to collect me, you'll allow me to make a phone call and… then you were to abduct me again,"

Caleb swallowed hard.

Bettie just shook her head. "What were you going to make me say in that phone call? That I was safe and going to be dropped off in one location then take me to another?"

Serenity grabbed Caleb's arm. Bettie cocked her head at that. It was a strange move to make. In Bettie's experience, at this point the partner of the accused always tried to make them confirm that they didn't do it.

But Caleb wasn't doing that in the slightest.

"Or are you on the take too?" Graham asked Serenity.

She laughed. Yet Bettie knew it was a strange nervous laugh.

Bettie watched Graham as he took out his handcuffs and did a citizen's arrests, and Bettie sent off the recording to a number of different locations so it was backed up at least ten times. Then she *accidentally* sent it to a local newspaper just for good measure.

As Graham started to lead Caleb and Serenity away, Bettie waved her hand to stop him.

"One more question," Bettie said, "you were going to take me to Willow Fisher for some reason. Why? And where are they?"

Caleb smiled. "That two questions,"

Graham tightened the cuffs. "Answer her,"

"He doesn't know," Serenity said. "He was meant to meet me, transfer you into my custody and I was to take you somewhere,"

"Where?" Bettie said, coldly.

"Go fuck yourself," Serenity said.

Bettie laughed and took Serenity's phone. "It's a shame when your phone slips out your pocket,"

With that Bettie simply walked away, she knew Graham was going to drop them off at the police station, explain what had happened and show the police the recording. But Bettie just hoped that would give her enough time to find where Willow Fisher was.

But now Bettie knew Willow Fisher wanted her, Bettie was starting to become terrified.

CHAPTER 18
2nd April 2022
Canterbury, England

Back at Bettie's office, Graham and Bettie both sat around her wooden table looking over at the data Bettie had cracked from Serenity's phone. Graham hated that cops were involved in criminal activity, and now he had to stop Willow and Mr Jones.

"The only texts from her phone," Bettie said, "are too unregistered numbers,"

Graham rolled his eyes. This isn't what they needed, even after all the tortuous paperwork and explaining he had to do when he took the two cops into custody and the prison cell. Graham still had little clue where the pair were meant to take Bettie.

"Wait," Graham said, "what if we're looking at this all wrong?"

"How so?" Bettie asked.

"Well, we're looking at texts and emails about the location of the drop-off. What if we need to look at other activity on the phone?"

Bettie smiled. "Of course. Even if Serenity had been sitting in the car ten minutes waiting for me to arrive. She might have used social media or something,"

"Exactly, and we can trace that. Allowing us to know where we can start to look for a hiding spot for a very private woman," Graham said.

Bettie flicked through the phone and bit her lip. Graham couldn't take his eyes off her, she was so attractive when she was concentrating.

"Here," Bettie said, "Serenity turned on her location and went on social media about the time Mr Harman, aka Caleb tried to free me. Then…"

Bettie busted out laughing and showed Graham the phone. Graham couldn't believe he was staring at the Maps app on her phone with the route to a little cottage in the middle of nowhere.

"She made it easy for us," Graham said.

Bettie shook her head. "What if… do you think this is another deception?"

Graham slowly shook his head. He wasn't sure. Everything in this from the beginning had been one massive deception with Willow Fisher, but Graham wouldn't be surprised if that wasn't her true name.

"No," Graham said. "It makes no sense this would be a deception. But the drug connection is still concerning me?"

"Same," Bettie said.

Graham shook his hands in the air. "We know

New Horizons dropped Willow in favour of geology. She breaks into the company. Caleb and Serenity investigate it, Willow brides them and they come cops on the take,"

Bettie nodded. "Then Willow realises the company will not take her back. So she blackmails Arlo to steal the rock, and Willow hires me to back up her story about the blackmail threats to make her look innocent in case something goes wrong-"

Graham cocked his head. "Why you?"

He could see Bettie was about to say it was because she was the best. Graham was never going to say she was wrong, she was the best, and he wasn't just saying that because they slept together. It was fact.

Then Bettie frowned. "I was played wasn't I?"

"And Phryne giving you a hard time only made it easier. Then Fisher blackmailed Phryne to make her keep verbally assaulting you. You were distracted," Graham said.

"Not only was I played? I don't see how the rock got into the drug suppliers hands?" Bettie said, getting out her own phone and dialling someone.

"Who you calling?"

"Skylar. Need to ask Arlo who he handed the rock to,"

Graham looked away as Bettie started talking to Skylar. It was just a strange habit he had formed over the years, but whatever the answer Graham wasn't sure it was going to make sense.

Logically Graham would have imagined Arlo would have to deliver the rock to Willow directly, because she was a very private woman. She wouldn't want too many people knowing about this, so Graham couldn't believe she would hire drug suppliers to deliver her the rock. That would only make her criminal activities more widely known.

"Thanks Skylar," Bettie said and turned to Graham. "It turns out Arlo was meant to hand the rock over to someone who we would never expect. And Arlo was assured tens of times apparently that the rock would be delivered to Willow,"

Graham smiled. "Who?"

"You already meet him apparently. Dr Albie Peterson,"

"What!" Graham shouted. "That makes no sense. He's far too anal about geology and making money from geology for him to risk everything,"

Bettie opened up her laptop and Graham saw she was doing a credit check on the good Doctor.

"He might not have cared too," Bettie said. "The credit check was bad enough, but look at this court filing from New Horizons two months ago,"

Graham came round and stood next to Bettie. It turned out the publishing company had paid the good doctor three million pounds to produce the geology products. But after the theft, New Horizons had tried to recreate the products, yet Albie refused.

Leaving New Horizons no choice but to sue him as he refused to repay the advance. The advance he had already spent.

Graham was shocked that Albie could be this reckless with the money.

"We thinking he didn't want to risk his reputation by stealing it himself?" Graham asked.

"Exactly," Bettie said. "I guess that Willow made him an offer and he became part of the plan. Do you think she would let him have his money?"

Graham smiled and laughed a little. "Come on Bettie. He's a doctor of geology. He's a smart man. He knew Willow would never give him his money, so…"

Bettie stood up and wrapped her arms around Graham. He liked that. A lot.

"Come on Gra. I think if you interview Albie you'll find he knows the drug suppliers. They were probably keeping the rock safe for him, until he could guarantee Willow would give him his money,"

Graham kissed Bettie. This was why they made such a good team, and she had to be right.

"Now my smart man," Bettie said in amongst more kissing. "I think we have Willow to catch and some drug suppliers to hunt,"

Graham kissed her and led her out of the office. She couldn't be more right.

And Graham was looking forward to finally capturing these criminal masterminds.

CHAPTER 19
2nd April 2022
2 Miles Outside Canterbury, England

As Bettie and Graham walked up to a large abandoned looking stone cottage with horrible cracked stone walls and windows. Bettie realised she hated this place with a passion.

She hated it even more when she saw there was no front door, so her and Graham simply walked in.

Bettie knew the other police officers would be here soon, so they ideally needed to be quick about this.

Bettie went through a narrow hallway with white wallpaper peeling off the walls, and judging by the little rooms that shot off the hallway, no one had lived here for a long, long time.

The hallway continued into a large surprisingly modern kitchen area with a modern stove, fridge and a massive wooden table with two people sitting round it.

Bettie smiled as she saw the horrible and utterly foul Willow Fisher in her disgusting black dress, and Mr Jones in his butler uniform. They were both merely sitting there with a mug of warm coffee each.

Bettie hated both of them for that alone. She really wanted to drink coffee, but she was never going to risk the baby.

"Mistress!" Mr Jones shouted, and they both looked at Bettie and Graham.

The sound of police sirens filled the air as more officers turned up outside.

"Why those wet ends tell you?" Willow asked.

Bettie smiled and shook her head. Now she fully believed this was the real Willow Fisher. She wasn't some amazing self-help person, she was nothing more than a cold, calculating person who didn't really care for anyone else.

And Bettie had no doubt she was somewhere on the psychotic scale. Bettie had never met someone so calculating, meticulous and utterly foul to everyone else.

Mr Jones started coughing.

More and more.

He gasped.

Graham rushed over to him.

Bettie dialled 999.

She ordered an ambulance.

Yet when she put the phone down, Bettie couldn't believe how much Willow was smiling at her. She wasn't trying to help Mr Jones whatsoever, and that only confirmed her suspicions. Willow didn't care about anyone, and Bettie knew she only saw people as playthings or objects to be used in some greater plan.

Bettie marched over to the table and Graham managed to keep Mr Jones breathing.

"Why?" Bettie asked with a smile.

Willow got up. "Because my dearest Miss English, I do not like people being better than me. You are arrogant, you were so pleased to hear we thought you were the best. You were easy,"

Bettie shook her head. She didn't want to be hearing this, but at least she knew the truth.

Willow Fisher didn't have a reason for picking her. Not really. Because that was the crazy thing about psychopaths they created such plans and dreams and myths for themselves that at the end of the day, all their so-called reasons were merely fantasy.

"I enjoyed our game Miss English. You were fun to play with, but do know I do not want to play again,"

Bettie simply nodded her head. She had never wanted to play in the first place, but at least (she really, really hoped) Willow Fisher would be sectioned and she would never be a threat to anyone again.

As the police officers came in and Graham told them to arrest Willow, and the ambulance crew helped Mr Jones who was now coughing and struggling to breathe. Bettie simply walked away.

She had solved her case, and hopefully helped

Graham too.

But as much as she wanted to forget this case, she knew she wouldn't.

And now she thought about it, Bettie wasn't sure that was such a bad thing.

Now Bettie had to check on something far, far more important.

The major difference between her and Willow Fisher.

Family and the people she loved with all her heart.

CHAPTER 20
2nd April 2022

Canterbury, England

After Graham had arrested both Willow Fisher and Mr Jones, he had interrogated Albie Peterson and he had thankfully given him the names of the drug suppliers. Leading to even more arrests.

Graham still hated all the paperwork involved, but at least he wasn't on suspension now and he really did love that.

As Graham walked along a long wide corridor with rather nice blue wallpaper that was starting to peel off at the edges, he couldn't help but look behind him at the massive grey door he had just left from.

That idiot police captain had really showed Graham the extent of the police… dodginess of recent days. It turned out that Caleb Young and Officer Simpson were not being dismissed as police officers or even investigated.

Graham had no idea how the police captain had

managed that considering Bettie had sent the recordings to the Police Watchdog, but he had. So now those two dangerous and corrupt police officers were back on the streets.

The smell of citrus, apple pie and other sweet treats filled the air as Graham passed a little kitchen area filled with other police officers who were talking and laughing and smiling at each other. He knew some of the officers in there, and he liked them.

And that was the truly awful thing about Young and Simpson. They truly were in the minority of officers who were homophobic, corrupt and just awful people. But they still managed to spoil it for the rest of them, because Sean had always been right.

Graham didn't know how the police were meant to reassure gays, people of colour and all the minorities the police served them too. But he wanted to find out, he wanted to protect everyone, not only for those people, yet because he truly believed it is what his kid would want.

He didn't want his kid growing up in a world where the police were viewed with suspicion and were treated as the bad guys for the actions of a few. Graham really wanted his kid to trust, love and respect the police. Not out of fear like so many minority groups do, but out of real respect.

And Graham knew that he had to start this change, by showing he respected all of them.

It turned out someone had recorded the public fight earlier between him and Officer Simpson and it was now a viral sensation. Graham was now known as some kind of protector of the innocent, or whatever the comment sections called him.

He didn't really care. He only cared that he was protecting the innocent, and now with the drug suppliers in jail Canterbury and Kent were a bit safer than they were yesterday morning.

Graham loved that.

Yet there was still one other thing that bugged Graham from that meeting with the police captain only moments ago. Apparently Graham was making enemies in the police by going against his fellow officers and showing the police's fake nature.

Graham denied it completely. He wasn't going against the police in the slightest. It was the other homophobic officers that were going against the values, principles and honour of the police.

The police captain didn't believe him.

So Graham knew he had to be more careful in truth. He had read stories like this too many times for comfort, officers that had showed the police up and found themselves disgraced a few months later.

He had to be very careful.

Graham saw a tall beautiful woman with the cutest little baby bump standing at the very end of the corridor, and that said everything to him.

Bettie was never going to let anything happen to him, and even if Graham wanted to sort out the police captain, Young and Simpson that was well and truly tomorrow's problem.

For now he just wanted to go home, love his wife and make sure the people in his life were okay. After all, they had all just had a very short and traumatic two days.

And family was the most important thing to Graham.

Far more important than the police.

CHAPTER 21
2nd April 2022
Canterbury, England

Bettie slowly sat down at her wonderful wooden chair and flat out loved her office in the heart of Canterbury. With the open window Bettie loved listening to the wonderful talking, laughing and shouting of the university students that pounded the pavement below.

The air smelt amazing of pies, bread and doughnuts from the local bakery. Bettie couldn't believe how lucky she was to be alive, happy and healthy. The past two days might have been strange and probably the weirdest case she had ever had.

But she loved it.

It was probably the first case Bettie had ever that had allowed her to explore her entire family and take them along for the ride, and surprisingly enough they all said they had enjoyed it.

Bettie kissed Graham's strong muscular arm as

he wrapped it around her and pulled her close. Then Bettie smiled at her beautiful sister that still looked blackened and bruised, but at least her swallowed jaw looked better, and Phryne was now on pain medication.

Then there was Sean sitting next to Phryne smiling and looking so amazing. Bettie was so lucky to have them all with her, protecting her and just being her family. They had all been so helpful and amazing these past two days, and Bettie dreaded to think what would have happened with them.

When the smell of custard started to enter the office, Bettie felt herself start to gag and she pointed to the window. Graham walked over and closed it.

Bettie didn't want to be sick today, or any day for that matter.

As Graham, Sean and Phryne told a few jokes about the hospital and apparently a very hand-ies male nurse. Bettie smiled but gently rubbed her baby bump.

It had been such a strange couple of days filled with masterful deceptions and some weird moves by the criminals. Bettie never would have imagined that Willow was a psychopath, but she was evaluated and sectioned never to be seen again.

Mr Jones was treated and it turned out that Willow Fisher had always planned to kill him after he had outlived his usefulness. And now Mr Jones was more than willing to plea guilty and explain everything to the police about the criminal acts of Willow spreading over five years.

Bettie had said that the police seemed interested, but after Graham had told her about Young and Simpson. She wasn't sure.

And she really understood why he was so annoyed about it all. She too wanted their kid to live in a world where the police were already the good guys to other people who weren't white, straight men. But things took time to change, and Bettie couldn't help but feel like Graham would be out of the police sooner or later.

So she made a note to herself to watch the police captain, Young and Simpson for a while and record everything little mistake they made.

Just in case.

Bettie hoped if the three of them wanted to get Graham out of the police, it would fail. Not only because of her and her family's determination, but because of a new political ally to. It turned out after watching the news a little while ago, Skylar Mason was now Justice Secretary for the UK Government, Bettie wasn't sure what that meant practically.

Yet theoretically it meant an ally in the halls of power in case things went wrong for an innocent person like Graham. Bettie wasn't sure, but only time would tell.

Bettie smiled as she felt the baby kick gently and guided Graham's hand so he could feel it too. She damn well loved him.

And Bettie was extremely grateful to him that

what Arlo Mason did for Willow would never enter official records and it turned out he was bisexual and now good friends with Sean and Harry, and Arlo stealing Harry's ID was now a joke amongst them.

At least Arlo's life didn't need to be destroyed because of one psychopath's actions. That really made Bettie happy. As well as if Arlo's theft couldn't be used in official channels then it meant the good doctor Albie Peterson was innocent too.

Graham hadn't been too happy about that, but Bettie convinced him otherwise. Albie wasn't going to steal again, and at the end of the day, he was just another victim of Willow's psychotic manipulation. Bettie didn't want him punished for that.

But what Bettie really cared about was discovering a secret bank account on Serenity's phone that belonged to Willow. Thankfully it included a good few tens of thousands that was mysteriously transferred to Bettie's account.

No one was going to notice, care or probably investigate that little transaction.

Sean's laughter, Phryne's gasping and Graham's chuckling pulled Bettie back to the room. It was amazing to see everyone so happy and now they could and would just relax after this case.

And now Bettie realised she really didn't care what Phryne had said only yesterday. She was damn good at her job and Bettie loved it, and when this baby came she was going to make sure it had the best childhood it possibly could.

Bettie wasn't going to get a proper job that was nine til five, five days a week that would make her miss her child's life. That was never going to happen.

So Bettie was always going to be a Private Eye, but a mother first and foremost, no matter what.

Phryne coughed and looked at Bettie.

"I'm... so-rr-y," Phryne said, forced.

Sean playfully hit her arm. "Mum. Do it properly,"

Phryne rolled her eyes and Bettie leant forward smiling.

"I'm sorry," Phryne said. "I never should have dismissed your career so quickly. Especially after you helped me out once or twice. I am sorry Bet,"

Bettie nodded and decided to play it up a little. After all that's what sisters are for, right?

"You know I was deeply hurt," Bettie said, smiling. "I think you should take us all out for dinner tonight at my favourite vegan restaurant,"

Bettie wished she had a camera as she watched all the colour, emotion and happiness drain from Phryne's face. Then Graham and Sean both stared at her too.

After a few moments, Phryne smiled. Not in a fake evil fashion like she must have done with clients, but a true loving smile.

"Fine, Bet. Let's go," Phryne said.

As everyone got up and Graham helped Bettie put her coat on and they all left for the restaurant, Bettie wrapped her arms around Graham and Sean.

She really did love them all and they were all the best family she could wish for.

Now they were going to have a wonderful night out on the town, relax and enjoy life.

Because that was what a great family did, and when your sister was paying for it all.

Why wouldn't you?

Keep up to date with exclusive deals on Connor Whiteley's Books, as well as the latest news about new releases and so much more!

Sign up for the Grab a Book and Chill Monthly newsletter, and you'll get one **FREE** ebook just for signing up: Agents of The Emperor Collection.

Sign Up Now!

https://dl.bookfunnel.com/f4p5xkprbk

About the author:

Connor Whiteley is the author of over 60 books in the sci-fi fantasy, nonfiction psychology and books for writer's genre and he is a Human Branding Speaker and Consultant.

He is a passionate warhammer 40,000 reader, psychology student and author.

Who narrates his own audiobooks and he hosts The Psychology World Podcast.

All whilst studying Psychology at the University of Kent, England.

Also, he was a former Explorer Scout where he gave a speech to the Maltese President in August 2018 and he attended Prince Charles' 70th Birthday Party at Buckingham Palace in May 2018.

Plus, he is a self-confessed coffee lover!

Other books by Connor Whiteley:

Bettie English Private Eye Series
A Very Private Woman
The Russian Case
A Very Urgent Matter
A Case Most Personal
Trains, Scots and Private Eyes
The Federation Protects

The Fireheart Fantasy Series
Heart of Fire
Heart of Lies
Heart of Prophecy
Heart of Bones
Heart of Fate

City of Assassins (Urban Fantasy)
City of Death
City of Marytrs
City of Pleasure
City of Power

Agents of The Emperor
Return of The Ancient Ones
Vigilance
Angels of Fire

The Garro Series- Fantasy/Sci-fi
GARRO: GALAXY'S END
GARRO: RISE OF THE ORDER
GARRO: END TIMES
GARRO: SHORT STORIES
GARRO: COLLECTION
GARRO: HERESY
GARRO: FAITHLESS
GARRO: DESTROYER OF WORLDS
GARRO: COLLECTIONS BOOK 4-6
GARRO: MISTRESS OF BLOOD
GARRO: BEACON OF HOPE
GARRO: END OF DAYS

Winter Series- Fantasy Trilogy Books
WINTER'S COMING
WINTER'S HUNT
WINTER'S REVENGE
WINTER'S DISSENSION

Miscellaneous:
RETURN
FREEDOM
SALVATION
Reflection of Mount Flame
The Masked One
The Great Deer

OTHER SHORT STORIES BY CONNOR WHITELEY

Blade of The Emperor
Arbiter's Truth
The Bloodied Rose
Asmodia's Wrath
Heart of A Killer
Emissary of Blood
Computation of Battle
Old One's Wrath
Puppets and Masters
Ship of Plague
Interrogation
Edge of Failure
One Way Choice
Acceptable Losses
Balance of Power
Good Idea At The Time
Escape Plan
Escape In The Hesitation
Inspiration In Need
Singing Warriors
Dragon Coins
Dragon Tea
Dragon Rider
Knowledge is Power
Killer of Polluters
Climate of Death
Sacrifice of the Soul
Heart of The Flesheater

Heart of The Regent
Heart of The Standing
Feline of The Lost
Heart of The Story
The Family Mailing Affair
Defining Criminality
The Martian Affair
A Cheating Affair
The Little Café Affair
Mountain of Death
Prisoner's Fight
Claws of Death
Bitter Air
Honey Hunt
Blade On A Train
City of Fire
Awaiting Death
Poison In The Candy Cane
Christmas Innocence
You Better Watch Out
Christmas Theft
Trouble In Christmas
Smell of The Lake
Problem In A Car
Theft, Past and Team
Embezzler In The Room
A Strange Way To Go
A Horrible Way To Go
Ann Awful Way To Go
An Old Way To Go

A Fishy Way To Go
A Pointy Way To Go
A High Way To Go
A Fiery Way To Go
A Glassy Way To Go
A Chocolatey Way To Go
Kendra Detective Mystery Collection Volume 1
Kendra Detective Mystery Collection Volume 2
Stealing A Chance At Freedom
Glassblowing and Death
Theft of Independence
Cookie Thief
Marble Thief
Book Thief
Art Thief

All books in 'An Introductory Series':
BIOLOGICAL PSYCHOLOGY 3RD EDITION
COGNITIVE PSYCHOLOGY THIRD EDITION
SOCIAL PSYCHOLOGY- 3RD EDITION
ABNORMAL PSYCHOLOGY 3RD EDITION
PSYCHOLOGY OF RELATIONSHIPS- 3RD EDITION
DEVELOPMENTAL PSYCHOLOGY 3RD EDITION
HEALTH PSYCHOLOGY
RESEARCH IN PSYCHOLOGY
A GUIDE TO MENTAL HEALTH AND TREATMENT AROUND THE WORLD- A GLOBAL LOOK AT DEPRESSION
FORENSIC PSYCHOLOGY
THE FORENSIC PSYCHOLOGY OF THEFT, BURGLARY AND OTHER CRIMES AGAINST PROPERTY
CRIMINAL PROFILING: A FORENSIC PSYCHOLOGY GUIDE TO FBI PROFILING AND GEOGRAPHICAL AND STATISTICAL PROFILING.
CLINICAL PSYCHOLOGY
FORMULATION IN PSYCHOTHERAPY
PERSONALITY PSYCHOLOGY AND INDIVIDUAL DIFFERENCES
CLINICAL PSYCHOLOGY REFLECTIONS VOLUME 1
CLINICAL PSYCHOLOGY REFLECTIONS VOLUME 2

CULT PSYCHOLOGY
Police Psychology

www.ingramcontent.com/pod-product-compliance
Lightning Source LLC
LaVergne TN
LVHW011839060526
838200LV00054B/4107